All the good are friends of one another.
—Zeno of Citium
333 B.C.–264 B.C.

You be good. See you tomorrow. I love you.
—Alex, an African grey parrot
1976–2007

The Desperate Adventures of
Zeno & Alya

JANE
KELLEY

SQUARE
FISH

Feiwel and Friends
New York

To my sister, Katharine, and my brother, Andy

SQUARE FISH

An Imprint of Macmillan
175 Fifth Avenue
New York, NY 10010
mackids.com

Square Fish and the Square Fish logo are trademarks of Macmillan and
are used by Feiwel and Friends under license from Macmillan.

Square Fish books may be purchased for business or promotional use.
For information on bulk purchases, please contact the Macmillan
Corporate and Premium Sales Department at (800) 221-7945 x5442
or by e-mail at specialmarkets@macmillan.com.

Library of Congress Cataloging-in-Publication Data Available
ISBN 978-1-250-06282-6 (paperback) / ISBN 978-1-4668-4854-2 (ebook)

Originally published in the United States by Feiwel and Friends
First Square Fish Edition: 2015
Book designed by Ashley Halsey
Square Fish logo designed by Filomena Tuosto

10 9 8 7 6 5 4 3 2 1

AR: 3.8 / LEXILE: 520L

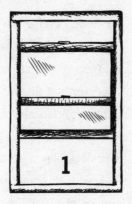

An alarm buzzed. A phone rang. Theme music from a news program played. A clock chimed ten, eleven, twelve, thirteen times. The alarm buzzed again louder and louder. And louder. No one turned it off. No one got up and put food in the shiny aluminum bowl that was, alas, completely empty.

The source of all these sounds rapped his beak on top of the bookcase. The house was silent for a moment, as if everything in it, even the walls of leather-bound books, hoped for a response. There was none. So the alarm buzzed, the phone rang, the music played, the clock chimed, the alarm buzzed, and a raucous voice proclaimed, "Zeno wants!"

Zeno was an African grey parrot. He could imitate sixty-three sounds and speak 127 words. Since those two were by far his favorites, he repeated them again, "Zeno wants!"

He flapped his gray wings and spread his tail that was as scarlet as the lining of a magician's cape. Then he flew over to the shiny aluminum bowl. He cocked his head to one side to see if his servant had filled it with food. There were no nuts, no fruits, no greens—nothing except Zeno's own reflection. He admired his sleek gray head and the sharp curve of his dark beak. Then he carefully lifted his left foot, grasped the rim of the bowl with his long gray toes, and flipped the bowl onto the floor. The metal clattered so delightfully on the hard wood that Zeno repeated the sound himself.

Then he paused, waiting to be praised and rewarded. No one said, "Brilliant bird." No one gave him an apple chunk. No one recorded the sound and the date in the notebook. No one said, "That makes sixty-four distinct sounds." And no one started a discussion of whether words should count as sounds. What was the difference between a sound and a word? Sounds had meanings, too. Didn't the buzz of the alarm mean "wake up"?

"Zeno wants," Zeno muttered mournfully. He flew over to perch on the desk so he could look down at his servant.

Dr. Agard was still sleeping on the floor. Zeno didn't understand this. Dr. Agard was a man of regular habits. He had never lain down on the floor for even a moment in the twenty years that he had been Zeno's servant. He had certainly never slept there.

The real phone rang. Zeno cocked his head and glared at the black rectangle. It rang seventeen times. Dr. Agard didn't get up to answer it.

Zeno made the sound of the buzzing alarm again. This was always very effective at waking up Dr. Agard, even when it was the middle of the night. However, nothing was as it should be.

Dr. Agard hadn't even put away his papers before taking his nap. He was always careful to keep them where Zeno couldn't get them. Several stacks were on the desk, including one that Dr. Agard had described as final exams. You see, in addition to being Zeno's servant, Dr. Agard was also a professor of Greek literature at Brooklyn College. He had named Zeno after a Greek philosopher. He often quoted the human Zeno to the parrot Zeno.

"Extravagance is its own destroyer," Zeno squawked. He waited for Dr. Agard to reward him for saying what the human Zeno said. There was no response. Surely it was extravagant of Dr. Agard to lie on the floor instead of feeding Zeno.

"Pfft," Zeno muttered. He put his foot on the stack of final exams and used his beak to tear a long strip off the top paper. This was one of Zeno's favorite things to do. He loved the feel of the paper in his mouth, loved the little bit of resistance from the paper, and then the soft sighing sound as the paper abandoned itself to Zeno's will. *Rip, rip, rip, rip.* What could be more satisfying than to turn a flat white sheet into a muddle of curls?

Zeno glanced at Dr. Agard again. He still hadn't moved. Zeno didn't understand this. Usually Dr. Agard would rush over at the first little rip, waving his hands and shouting, "Those are my papers, Zeno. Mine."

Well, perhaps they were Dr. Agard's. However, Zeno didn't see why he wanted them. He never did anything interesting with them. He just held them in his hand. Occasionally he made marks like bird tracks with that short stick, which Zeno wasn't supposed to gnaw, either. What was enjoyable about that? Nothing. In fact, Dr. Agard often moaned as he was marking the papers. Sometimes he would say things like, "You could have written a better essay than this, Zeno." And Zeno would nod his head several times yes yes yes. Even though he couldn't really claim to know the words "essay" or "written," he did know that he could have done a better job at whatever it was because he was, of course, Zeno.

Finally all the papers had been shredded. Dr. Agard hadn't rescued a single one.

"Mine?" Zeno said.

He turned his head upside down to stare at Dr. Agard. Then he turned his head the other way to ponder the situation from that point of view. What was Dr. Agard doing down there? Dr. Agard often told Zeno that Zeno had to control his emotions if he wanted to achieve wisdom. This was called being stoic. The human Zeno was supposed to be very good at that and at accepting his fate. The parrot Zeno wondered if that was why Dr. Agard was lying there? Had he found wisdom by not being angry at Zeno?

"Pfffft," Zeno muttered.

If that were true, being stoic didn't seem like a good thing. Of course Zeno was delighted that Dr. Agard wasn't angry. However, Dr. Agard didn't seem happy, either. And Dr. Agard seemed to have forgotten all about sharing their Sunday morning treat.

Unlike his human namesake, Zeno the bird never suffered in silence. "Zeno wants!" he squawked.

And what did Zeno want? Since you are no doubt much better at understanding your feelings than poor Zeno, you know that Zeno wanted Dr. Agard to get up. He wanted the life they had shared for twenty years to continue. He wanted not to feel alone in the house. He wanted to be rid of that little throbbing knot of fear and dread in his stomach. He wanted . . .

"Banana nut!" Zeno squawked.

Well, he wasn't the only one who thought everything would be all right if he could just eat his favorite food.

Sharing banana-nut muffins was one of their rituals. Unfortunately Dr. Agard had decided to take a nap on the floor like a stoic instead of going out to get their special Sunday treat.

Zeno flapped down and stood right next to Dr. Agard's head.

Dr. Agard didn't move.

"Banana nut?" Zeno muttered mournfully.

The phone rang again.

Dr. Agard didn't move.

Zeno rubbed the side of his beak against Dr. Agard's finger—the one Dr. Agard used to scratch the top of Zeno's head, right in the dark gray patch of feathers, between the pale gray circles that surrounded his yellow eyes. Dr. Agard always stroked Zeno's head as he said that Zeno was the most beautiful, brilliant bird in all of Brooklyn.

"Booful, briyant bird," Zeno muttered.

The doorbell rang—the real one. Then someone knocked on the door. "Dr. Agard? Dr. Agard?"

The knocking turned to banging.

"Dr. Agard!"

Zeno recognized the voice of Dr. Agard's assistant. There had been many over the years. Zeno never liked them. They didn't seem to understand that since Dr. Agard was Zeno's servant, the servants of Dr. Agard must be Zeno's servants, too. The current assistant frequently referred to Zeno as "that bird." He had yelled at Zeno in a most un-stoic-like fashion just because Zeno had ripped open the assistant's backpack to help himself to a packet of mixed nuts.

"Dr. Agard? I'm opening the door."

The locks turned. The door opened. Zeno flapped his

wings and flashed his scarlet tail feathers. "BRAWWWK!" Zeno squawked, ready to defend Dr. Agard against these intruders.

The assistant and two other men in blue clothes rushed into the room.

"Get that bird out of here," the assistant shouted.

That bird? The assistant should have learned Zeno's name by now. Dr. Agard had told the assistant often enough.

"Zeno," Zeno squawked. "Booful, briyant Zeno."

The humans weren't listening. One actually shoved Zeno away from Dr. Agard. Zeno was so shocked by this rough treatment that he flew up to the bookshelf. He pulled a book of Greek tragedies off the top shelf and dropped it to the floor. *Plop.* He kept pulling books until he had cleared the entire shelf. *Plop, plop, plop, plop.*

The men in blue knelt by Dr. Agard. They loosened his clothes, poked him with needles, stuck tubes in his arms, and covered his face with a mask.

And still Dr. Agard didn't move.

After several frantic moments, the men in blue stopped what they were doing and became almost as motionless as Dr. Agard. "That's all we can do," one said.

The assistant nodded and hid his mouth behind his hand.

The men in blue gently lifted Dr. Agard onto a little cot, covered him with a white cloth, and wheeled him out the front door.

Zeno was shocked. Where were they taking Dr. Agard?

"Mine!" he squawked, because of course Dr. Agard was *his* servant. He flew out the front door after them and perched on the lowest branch of an oak tree.

The assistant hovered close by as the men in blue put Dr. Agard in the back of a white van. They slammed the doors shut. Bang.

Zeno watched the van drive up the street and disappear around the corner. He looked at the door to the house. Should he go back inside? What for? His dishes were empty. The papers were shredded. And Dr. Agard, his devoted servant, had gone.

"Zeno want?" Zeno muttered.

No one responded to him. So Zeno flew off to make his own way in the great wide world.

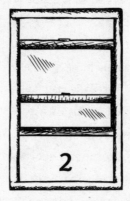

2

Being outside was so exhilarating for Zeno that he got out of breath after only flying five blocks. He wasn't used to that much exercise. Of course, he had been free to fly wherever he wanted in Dr. Agard's house. However, he usually only wanted to fly the short distance between his stand and his aluminum dishes.

He perched on a tree branch and paused to look around him. The buildings in this part of Brooklyn were all very similar. They were made of brown stone, about four stories tall. Each one was squeezed against its neighbor, with a short flight of stairs between the front door and the sidewalk. The tiny front yards contained flower gardens. Tall trees arched their branches above the streets. These trees were just beginning to get their leaves. It was spring, although Zeno understood little about the seasons because the temperature was constant inside Dr. Agard's house.

A breeze ruffled his feathers. "Pfft," Zeno muttered. He would have to set them right again as soon as he found food. He was extremely hungry.

Zeno had never actually had to find his meals before. He had been fed first by his own parents, and then, after his capture, by various humans until Dr. Agard had been given the honor of becoming Zeno's servant.

Now Dr. Agard had gone away. This was not unusual. Dr. Agard took his papers and went away nearly every day. This time, Dr. Agard had left Zeno without making sure his dishes were full and Zeno had cardboard to gnaw—and without saying, "Good-bye, Zeno, you beautiful, brilliant bird."

"Booful, briyant," Zeno said. He would have to feed himself. He wasn't worried about that. For one thing, if he were in charge of finding his own food, he intended to eat only the things he liked. At the top of that list were banana-nut muffins.

"Banana nut!" Zeno squawked.

He examined the branch upon which he sat. Tiny green leaves had pushed their way up from the brown bark. Obviously this tree was not the source of the banana-nut muffins. He flew farther down the block. He saw trees with pink buds, old brown leaves, and white flowers. Where were the ones with banana-nut muffins?

He flew over a roof and perched in the branches of a pine tree that grew in the backyard between the rows of houses. From a distance, the large brown cones seemed promising, but they weren't muffins, either.

"Pffft," Zeno muttered. How could this be? Dr. Agard must have gotten the muffins from somewhere. And food grew on trees. Zeno was certain of this. Buried beneath his 127 words and sixty-three sounds was a parrot memory. It had been handed down for generations, along with the scarlet feathers of his tail and the ability to talk. Parrots found food on trees. Of course the food they found was a particular kind of palm nut that grew on a type of tree that would never survive the winter in Brooklyn. Still, Zeno felt confident that the food he craved also grew on trees. Where else could it be?

He flew on and on, trying to match the parrot memory to what he observed. Wasn't the row of buildings like a cliff? Wasn't the street with its rush of cars like a river? Wasn't the lamppost just as branchless as a palm tree?

On and on, he flew, and around and around. He didn't dare stray too far, just in case Dr. Agard came back. At any moment, Zeno expected Dr. Agard to appear, holding the white paper bag decorated with blue flowers. "So sorry to be late, old chum. Here's our Sunday treat. Banana-nut muffins!"

But that, as you know, wasn't going to happen.

"Banana nut," Zeno muttered mournfully. He flapped

13

down to perch on the low branch of a pear tree and bent over to preen.

The dark gray feathers that adorned his neck had gotten quite ruffled. He always found comfort in stroking his beautiful feathers. He had never been in a situation quite as stressful as this. His hunger had reached an entirely new level of emptiness. He wasn't sure what to do about that. He might have to tug at every single feather before he felt like himself again.

A high-pitched voice below him said, "Look, Mom. It's a parrot."

Zeno turned sideways to look at the human. There were two of them, both female. Neither one had the glass circles in front of their eyes like Dr. Agard did. The smaller one had spoken to Zeno. She danced around and pointed at him with a purple circle on the end of a stick.

The girl put the circle in her mouth. Was this food? Would Zeno like to eat it? He never saw shiny purple food before. He leaned closer to get a better look.

"That looks like an African grey parrot," the woman said.

Zeno bobbed his head up and down several times, pleased to be recognized. Since Dr. Agard had gone, per- haps this human might enjoy being Zeno's servant?

"Can we take him home?" the girl said.

"Oh, no," the woman said quickly.

"Why not? He looks lonely," the girl said.

Zeno blinked. "Lonely" wasn't one of his one 127 words. He had no idea what it meant. He knew he preferred to be described as brilliant and beautiful.

"Polly want a cracker?" the girl said.

"Pfft," muttered Zeno. Why did humans always ask him about Polly? Who was Polly? Why on earth would Polly want crackers? The one Zeno tried had crumbled into tasteless powder with his first chomp.

"I'm sure he's someone's pet," the woman said.

"Pet?" Zeno squawked. Dr. Agard always scolded anyone who called Zeno a pet.

"He talked, Mommy, did you hear him say 'pet'?" the girl said. "Can we keep him?"

"No, dear, he didn't really talk. He just imitated what I said. He's a bird. He has no idea what words actually mean," the woman said.

"Brawwk!" Zeno flapped his wings vigorously. No idea? How dare the woman say that. He knew what words meant. He knew plenty of things. He was confident he knew much more than the woman. Even if he didn't exactly know where to find banana-nut muffins, she probably didn't, either.

"He can't really think for himself," the woman said.

"Better to trip with the feet than with the tongue." Zeno repeated one of the human Zeno's sayings. Dr. Agard often used that quote to scold his assistant for speaking foolishly.

"Did you hear that?" the girl said.

"That just proves my point. His owner taught him those words. A parrot couldn't possibly know what they mean," the woman said.

Of course Zeno knew. Sort of. Even if he couldn't explain it. Well, he knew that the quote always made the assistant shut up for a while.

"What *does* it mean?" the girl said.

"It means we better hurry or we'll be late for your violin lesson," the woman said.

She took the girl's hand—the one without the purple circle. Together they ran down the street.

As soon as the humans had gone, Zeno thought of what he *should* have said to them.

"Zeno not pet!" he squawked.

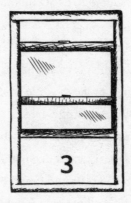

Zeno flew way up over one of Brooklyn's brownstone houses. From a window on the third floor of that house, a girl named Alya watched something gray streak across the sky. She was too far away to hear Zeno squawk. Was that a bird? she wondered. No, probably just another jet.

Her mother came in the room. Mrs. Logan straightened Alya's pillow and tucked the blankets tightly between the mattress and the railing that surrounded the bed. The bed could move in mysterious ways. Up and down and jiggling inside. Alya didn't like it. Not at all. She had said over and over again, she didn't need a hospital bed, she didn't want a hospital bed, she wasn't in a hospital. But Mrs. Logan said Alya couldn't sleep in the hammock anymore. When the bed came and filled the room, she had to lie down on it. There was no place else for her to be.

It's a shame you have to meet Alya now. You'd never guess how clever she used to be at climbing trees. Or inventing new games with a soccer ball. And you can't know what her real laugh sounded like. The one that exploded from her belly—not the whispery "ha ha" that barely tiptoed past her lips. It's hard to laugh while you're lying in bed.

You're probably wondering why she didn't get up. Alya wondered that, too. Why had her body betrayed her?

The official diagnosis was leukemia. A few months ago, doctors had done blood tests and found traitorous cells that only pretended to be the kind that fought infections. Those cells got in the way and kept Alya's real blood cells from doing their jobs. The doctors had used chemotherapy to kill the cancer cells. A fierce battle had been fought inside Alya. Unfortunately many useful cells had been destroyed, too—including the roots for Alya's dark cloud of curls. Those treatments had ended. Her hair was even starting to grow back. But for some reason her muscles still didn't want to do hardly anything anymore.

"There now," Mrs. Logan said in her most cheerful voice.

Mrs. Logan stroked Alya's head for the 9,578th time. "Your hair's growing back so soft. Just like when you were a baby."

"I'm not a baby," Alya said, and then bit her lip because she knew she sounded very much like one.

A distant bell rang.

"Someone's at the door. I bet it's Liza and Kiki." Mrs. Logan ran down the stairs.

Alya was stuck in her bed. Too late, she remembered that the plaid cap she wore for visitors was a million miles away on top of her dresser, next to the gray corner.

The corner really was the color of gloom. Her bedroom walls had been pale yellow ever since her parents hadn't known if she would be a boy or a girl. After Alya turned ten, she started planning how to redecorate her room. It took months to decide—well, Alya was busy. First there was soccer season. Then her friend Liza thought they should all be in the school play. Then Kiki signed them up for the swim team. Then they all went to sleepaway camp. In the fall, when the Logans vacationed in Puerto Rico, Alya discovered what she wanted—blue sky, crashing waves, tropical flowers, palm trees, and a real rope hammock to sleep in. She finished the waves and most of the sky before running out of blue paint. Then Alya's body had betrayed her and no one had time to even think about getting any more.

She heard her mom's voice from far away. "Come in, come in. It's so nice of you to come. Alya will be so happy to see you."

Alya thought how good at lying her mom had gotten. Of course, practice made perfect. Mrs. Logan never told the whole truth anymore. Every day she said stuff like how great Alya was doing and how cute Alya looked in a cap.

"We forgot to bring Alya's homework," Kiki said.

"I'd like to forget mine." Liza giggled.

"I'm sure she won't mind," Mrs. Logan said.

They all laughed.

"We did bring her a book," Kiki said.

"That's wonderful. Well, go on up. You know the way," Mrs. Logan said.

The girls did. They had been running up and down these steps for almost as many years as Alya herself had. Only this time her friends' footsteps told Alya what their words hadn't said. One set marched straight up. A soldier doing her duty. Sturdy sneakers. That would be Kiki. The other pair of feet scuffled along. One step forward and two steps back. Liza in her ballerina flats.

"Come on," Kiki said.

"I got something in my shoe," Liza said.

They paused at the second floor—where Alya's parents' bedroom was and the little office for her dad.

Alya wondered if she had time to get the cap. She put her hands on the railing and tried to pull herself toward the end of the bed. Her muscles quivered. She seemed to feel a thousand tiny ropes inside her arms break one at a time. She lied back down on the bed. She shut her eyes. It would be so much better if she didn't have to *see* them see her being bald. Of course they knew she had lost her hair. The cap didn't cover all the places where her curls used to be. But when she wore the cap, at least they could all pretend that everything was normal.

"Stop stalling," Kiki said.

"I'm not. I know there's a stone in there. I just can't find it."

"Let me have the shoe."

Bang bang bang. Kiki must have hit the shoe against the railing. The sound stopped and the footsteps started again.

And stopped.

"Now what?" Kiki said.

Whispering.

Kiki whispered back. Only her whispering was never as quiet as Liza's. "You don't have to plan what you're going to say. You never did before."

No, Liza never did before. However, things change. As Alya knew perfectly well.

So she planned what she was going to say. She planned how she was going to tell them that they didn't have to visit her ever again.

"Hi Alya!" Kiki said.

"Hi Alya!" Liza said.

"Hi Kiki. Hi Liza," Alya said.

Her friends had flushed cheeks. The wind had messed up Kiki's ponytail and changed the part in Liza's hair. They weren't wearing their coats. They must have shed them somewhere along the way. Soccer practice? Prospect Park?

The bench outside the corner store? Alya didn't want to think of all the places they could have been.

"It's so nice outside. It's a beautiful spring day. I just love spring, don't you? I think it's my favorite season," Liza said.

"Can I open the window? Then you could enjoy it, too," Kiki said.

"Sure," Alya said.

Kiki walked over to pull up the window. The breeze brought in the sounds of children playing somewhere. Kiki and Liza stood at the foot of the bed. They didn't look at Alya. Their eyes traveled all around the room like they were following a butterfly that zig-zagged over a meadow looking for someplace safe to rest, hurrying past the gray corner and the cap sitting oh-so-far away on the dresser, to finally land on the thing Kiki held in her own hand.

"We brought you a book," Kiki said.

"You might have already read it," Liza said.

"It's so good you could read it again." Kiki held it out over the railing.

Alya took the copy of *The Secret Garden*. The cover was green. A girl was running down a garden path, looking up at a red bird. "Thanks."

"*Have* you read it?" Liza said.

"Maybe." Alya put the book down on the bed. It was hard to remember things she had done before she got sick.

"We didn't bring you any homework. Sorry," Kiki said.

"Actually we didn't have much. Ms. McCusker is the

greatest teacher ever. She said that the best education we could get this weekend would be to go outside," Liza said.

"So why aren't you?" Alya said.

"We were in the park," Kiki said.

"And now we're visiting you." Liza smiled.

Alya smiled.

Kiki smiled.

"You should have seen. We were at the monkey bars? And Lenny was goofing around trying to act like a big gorilla. Swinging back and forth from one hand so he could scratch his stomach with the other. Then he fell. Bam. Right on his butt," Liza said.

"It was so funny. He actually bounced," Kiki said.

"It was so funny," Liza said again.

"You should have been there. You could have shown him how to do it. Remember that time you went back and forth ten times without stopping to rest?" Kiki said.

"Lenny bet you couldn't and he had to pay you five dollars," Liza said.

"Because you're the best," Kiki said.

Not anymore, Alya thought. The last time she tried to cross the bars, she had fallen. She crashed so hard she bruised her whole body. That was how her mom found out Alya was sick.

She shut her eyes. She felt her friends peering closer at her. She didn't open her eyes. She pretended she had fallen asleep.

"Alya?" Kiki said.

"I think she's sleeping," Liza whispered.

"Alya?" Kiki said.

"Don't wake her up. Let's just go," Liza whispered.

"Okay," Kiki whispered.

The girls tiptoed out of the room, but Alya could still hear Liza whispering to Kiki.

"She looks so scary without her hair."

"I wonder why she didn't wear her cap."

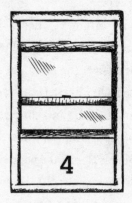

4

Mrs. Logan came in the bedroom carrying a red plate. "Why did the girls leave so soon? I was just bringing you all some muffins. They're banana nut. Your favorite."

Mrs. Logan held the plate right under Alya's nose. The three muffins looked like blobs of yellow glop. Alya sighed. After the treatments, nothing tasted the same to her. For some reason, the things she had loved the most tasted the worst of all.

"Don't you even want one little bite? Well, maybe you'll be hungry later." Mrs. Logan put the red plate on the table by the window. "Who opened the window?"

"Kiki," Alya said.

"It is a nice day. Spring is definitely in the air. But it would be terrible if you got sick. Aren't you chilly, sweetheart?"

Alya shook her head. She refused to admit she was cold. The old Alya never was.

"Just a few more minutes. Then I'll come back and shut it."

Mrs. Logan leaned over the railing to stroke Alya's head for the 9,579th time. Then she left the room.

Alya had never been the imagining sort of kid. Now that her body didn't do much, her mind drifted like a little boat with a torn sail, all alone on a wide sea. Strange things came up from those murky depths. Sometimes the traitorous cells floated around like purple balloons. Sometimes the food she couldn't eat rained down upon her like in *Cloudy with a Chance of Meatballs*. Mostly she saw the shadow of the monster who lurked in the gloomy corner, waiting, just waiting.

Suddenly there was a frantic flapping at her bedroom window. A new monster perched on the horizontal bars that were outside all windows to keep little children from accidently falling out. This monster spread its great gray wings and screeched, "Brawk!"

Actually it wasn't a monster at all. True, its ancestors had terrorized our planet, but this wasn't a terrible lizard otherwise known as a dinosaur. This was a large African grey parrot, whom you already know.

"Banana nut!" Zeno squawked. He was thrilled to have found the food he wanted most.

At first, Alya couldn't understand Zeno. The things she imagined didn't usually speak.

"Banana banana banana nut nut nut!" There wasn't just one, but three! He rapped his dark gray beak against the screen three times.

Finally she realized what the parrot was talking about. "Do you mean the muffins? You're right. They are banana nut."

"Mine!" Zeno squawked.

"How did you know what kind they were?" Alya was very impressed.

How did he know? Why, he was an expert on muffins, of course. He spread his wings and flashed his scarlet tail feathers. "Zeno wants!"

"Is that your name? Zeno?" Alya said.

Zeno bobbed his head, yes yes yes.

"What a great name," Alya said.

"Greek," Zeno corrected her.

"It's all Greek to me. My dad says that when he doesn't understand something. Which is pretty often." There was one particular Greek word that none of them understood—leukemia.

"It's all Greek to me," Zeno imitated Alya.

Alya smiled and made a small *heh, heh* sound, which was all that was left of her laugh.

Zeno cocked his head and waited for his reward. The

girl didn't move. Didn't she know she was supposed to give him the muffin now? He had done something clever. He blinked at her. What was the matter with the girl? She was a terrible servant. She obviously wasn't as intelligent as Dr. Agard. He rapped on the screen, the infuriating screen, which was the only thing between him and utter happiness. "Zeno wants!"

"You want me to open the screen?" Alya said.

Zeno nodded his head, yes yes yes.

"I can't. It's too far away. Besides, I'm sick," Alya said.

Sick was not one of Zeno's 127 words. He glared at Alya sternly with one yellow eye. He rapped his beak against the metal screen and squawked, "Try!"

Alya folded her arms across her chest. She most certainly would not. She was tired of trying. She was especially tired of being urged to try. Never hurts to try, people said. However, she knew quite well that it did hurt. It hurt when she couldn't do what she had once done. It hurt to be reminded of her weakness. It hurt to fail again and again. "It hurts."

"The wise are earnest in self-improvement," Zeno told her what the human Zeno had said.

"Don't tell *me* what to do. You don't even know what you're saying. You're just a dumb parrot," Alya said.

Zeno glared at her. He couldn't believe he had been insulted by a human again. However, the muffins were what mattered most. If the girl refused to be his servant, he would help himself. He hooked his beak around the edge of the screen.

"What are you doing? Stop that. You'll break it," Alya said.

Zeno tugged at the screen. His beak slipped off the metal. He bit through the mesh and hooked it again.

The bedroom door opened and Mrs. Logan rushed in. "Alya, what's the matter?"

"Look!" Alya pointed at the window.

Mrs. Logan gasped when she saw the parrot. She waved her hands and shouted, "Shoo!"

Zeno would have informed her that he wasn't a shoe, he was a parrot; however, his beak was busy. Just at that moment, he succeeded in yanking out the screen. It fell away from the window and landed in the branches of a pine tree. Zeno flapped his wings and praised himself. "Good parrot!"

He was extremely proud of his accomplishment—until Mrs. Logan slammed the window shut.

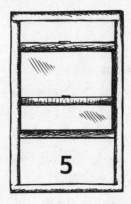

5

Zeno angrily rapped his beak against the glass. This woman wouldn't help him, either. She waved her hands at him several times. He rapped harder and harder until she picked up the muffins and carried them out of the room.

He stared at the girl in the bed. Why wasn't she doing anything? This puzzled him. Dr. Agard was always busy with his papers. The girl had a book beside her that she could have been enjoying. No one had gnawed its edges yet. And yet she just lay there.

"Try!" Zeno squawked again. Maybe the girl could run after the woman and get the muffins.

The girl looked at him with very sad brown eyes. "I'm sorry, I can't," she said. Then she turned her head away.

"Pfft," Zeno muttered. Something wasn't right. He turned his head completely upside down. Sometimes a new point of view helped him discover things, such as where Dr. Agard had hidden Zeno's treats. However, being upside down only made him feel queasy. And that reminded him that he was hungry.

He flapped away from the window and continued his search for something to eat. As he flew on and on without finding another muffin, each flap of his wings made him more frustrated. He got angry with Dr. Agard. Hadn't he caused all this trouble by sleeping on the floor and letting those strangers take him away? Why had Dr. Agard decided to be stoic? Was that why the girl hadn't tried to open the screen? Why did they think being stoic was a good thing? Wasn't it better to try? If Zeno didn't try, how would he ever find the banana-nut-muffin tree?

He came upon a tree full of brown balls. He perched on its branch. A short distance away, he noticed two squirrels chasing each other up one tree and down the next. Zeno knew about squirrels. He could see them from Dr. Agard's kitchen window. Dr. Agard often teased Zeno by saying he was going to give Zeno's nuts to the squirrels if Zeno didn't concentrate on learning new words. Of course Dr. Agard never did.

Now the squirrels were in the branches above Zeno. Were these the same squirrels? He couldn't tell. All squirrels looked alike. The squirrels were nibbling something they held with their front paws. What could it be? Zeno cocked his head. It was brown like the balls. If squirrels ate those, then Zeno better get one before the squirrels gobbled them all up. Zeno pulled himself up the tree with his beak and chomped down on a brown ball.

"Blawwk!" The ball was covered with spikes.

"Crit crit crit crit," the squirrels chattered and laughed.

"Blawk blawk blawk!" Zeno spluttered and spit and spit and spluttered. His tongue hurt so much he could barely talk.

The squirrels laughed until they tumbled out of that tree and scampered up another one.

Zeno's mouth was on fire. He flew up the street until he saw a puddle. It was dirty. A sparrow was bathing in it. Zeno was in too much pain to be fussy. As he drank from a mud puddle, he had to wonder if maybe, just maybe, he wasn't really the most beautiful, brilliant bird in all of Brooklyn.

Then Zeno saw a man. It was Dr. Agard! He was walking along the sidewalk on the far side of the street, carrying a very large white bag decorated with swirls of blue flowers. Zeno recognized it instantly. That bag could only have come from one place, and, what's more, that bag could only contain one thing.

"Banana nut!" Zeno squawked.

The man carrying the bag didn't seem to hear Zeno.

"Banana banana nut!" Zeno squawked even more loudly.

Had Dr. Agard lost his hearing? Zeno whistled and trilled his very best imitation of the theme song to Dr. Agard's favorite radio show. Zeno was always generously rewarded for that. The man didn't get the muffins out of the bag or reach into his pockets for nuts. He continued on around the corner.

Why wasn't Dr. Agard coming to beg his forgiveness? In the past, Dr. Agard had been extremely sorry whenever he arrived after Zeno's scheduled feeding time. Zeno stretched his wings and flew after the man to find out what was wrong. As Zeno got closer, he noticed that Dr. Agard had changed in other ways, too. He seemed shorter and rounder now. Instead of his brown sport coat, he was wearing a red sweatshirt, almost as vivid as the color of Zeno's tail. Zeno perched on the lowest branch of a pear tree. "Brawwk!"

The man stopped and took a step back, holding the bag in front of his chest. His eyes widened with terror. He waved his arm. "Get away from me, you crazy bird!"

What was the matter with Dr. Agard? Zeno was too hungry to figure it out. He extended his claws and snatched the bag away from the man. The bag tore. A cup and something wrapped in paper fell onto the sidewalk. Steaming black liquid splattered onto the man's blue jeans. The man screamed and ran away.

Zeno flapped down and stood next to his prize. The black liquid flowed toward the white paper. Zeno delicately plucked it up. Underneath it was a dark brown circle dotted with smaller colorful circles. Red, green, blue. Zeno had never seen a muffin look like that before. He let the paper fall.

"Banana nut?" Zeno muttered sadly.

He picked up his left foot to keep it away from the hot black liquid.

A flock of little brown birds fluttered down next to Zeno.

"Che che che che che?" they cheeped, which could be translated to mean, *Are you going to eat that?*

"Pfft," Zeno muttered. Of course he wasn't.

He flapped up to perch in a nearby pear tree. From there he watched the sparrows peck at the mess. The disappointment was almost more than he could bear. The man hadn't been Dr. Agard after all. How could Zeno have been wrong? He was never wrong.

The wind blew away the white paper bag. Zeno watched it roll down the sidewalk until all hope of a muffin was gone.

He observed those other birds greedily eating the crumbs until his empty stomach overcame his pride. He flapped down to the sidewalk. "Mine!" he squawked.

"Che che che," they cheeped, which meant, *We can share.*

Share? With sparrows? Zeno chased them away with a flash of his scarlet tail. He took a bite of the soggy mess that was left on the sidewalk. It tasted terrible. Still, he ate it because he had learned that not eating anything was much worse.

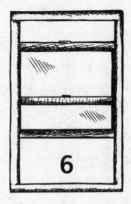

6

The book began promisingly enough, even though the hard cover pressed against the most tender part of Alya's belly. She kind of remembered that *The Secret Garden* was about a disagreeable little girl. Sure enough, the story started with Mistress Mary yelling at the servants. Alya found that refreshing. The setting was India, which had to be exotic. She couldn't wait to be carried far, far away from Brooklyn and her hateful bed. She read eagerly about the scarlet hibiscus flowers and Mem Sahib. Alya turned the page. She was hoping for a tiger. Didn't tigers prowl the countryside in India even now?

Then there it was, just like always. Inescapable. Inevitable. Spelled out in black and white.

The wailing grew wilder and wilder.

"What is it? What is it?" Mrs. Lennox gasped.
"Someone has died."

How could that author do this to her? Alya hurled the book across the room. It banged against the wooden floor.

Of course the possibility of death was always there—for everyone and everything. Only most people didn't have to think about it. Most people didn't have to take poison to prevent it. Nobody ever told Alya she might die. She just knew that her cancer was every bit as serious as what people did to her to try to get rid of it.

Still she tried hard not to stare at the gray corner of her room. Most of the time she succeeded in pretending it wasn't there. And then her friends (who didn't know any better) brought it to her in a book with a pretty cover.

Her brother, Parker, rushed into the room. "What's wrong? Are you okay? I heard a thump. I thought you fell."

Alya pointed to the railings that surrounded her.

"Oh. Right."

Parker stood by Alya's bed. Had he grown another inch that day? Or did he just seem taller since he was standing up and she was lying down?

"So what happened?" Parker leaned against the windowsill. He propped one foot up against the railing to get comfortable. Then he thought he shouldn't touch the hospital bed, so he quickly lowered his foot to the floor.

"Nothing." Now that her older brother was here, her

feelings seemed silly. "I just decided I didn't want to read right now."

He noticed the book on the floor. He picked it up and flipped through a few pages. "I remember this book. I could never figure out why that robin showed the girl the key."

"What key?" Alya hadn't read that far.

"The garden is all locked up because somebody died—I mean, did something stupid."

Alya pretended he hadn't said the word they never allowed themselves to speak.

"So this robin shows the girl the key that unlocks the Secret Garden. And that's what saves the girl."

"The robin?"

"Right. Like a robin would even know what a key was? I mean, I know it's a novel and everything, but still."

Parker let the book fall to the floor again. "If you want to read something good, I'll bring you some of my comic books."

"What if it were a different kind of bird? A smarter bird? Then would you think it could know how to save a girl? Like if it told you to do something, would you think you should?"

"A bird? Are you crazy?" Parker didn't say "crazy" in a mean way—just how a brother usually said it to his little sister. Only that wasn't quite how it felt to Alya.

"No. I'm not," Alya said.

"Course you're not." Parker kicked the book with his

foot until it disappeared under the bed. Alya wished she could ask him to take the book and its dying people to his room, but she couldn't because that *would* have been crazy.

Parker looked out the window, where everything was the way it was supposed to be, except there was a screen stuck in the branches of the pine tree. "There's that screen Mom says I'm supposed to get. You're the one who's good at climbing trees."

"I hope we don't need it anytime soon," Alya said.

Was Alya making a joke? Should he laugh? What if she wasn't joking? Parker stuck his hands in his pockets and thought hard for a way to change the subject. "That's pretty cool you saw a parrot, though. Did it talk?"

Alya nodded. Oh yes, it had.

"What did it say? 'Polly want a cracker'?" Parker laughed.

Alya shook her head.

"What then?"

"Just some words. He didn't know what he was saying."

Except she knew he did. He had known his name and that he wanted her muffin. He had known that she should have at least *tried* to give it to him.

"Got to go study for a biology test." Parker headed for the door. "Need me to get you anything?"

Alya shook her head.

"You sure? I could bring those comics. I got a new one the other day. Haven't even taken it out of the plastic. You could read it before I spill Frappuccino on it."

He was trying to help. There wasn't anything he could do. There wasn't anything anybody could do. Alya shook her head harder. She blinked several times.

"If you change your mind, call me. Throw a book or something, okay?"

"Okay," Alya said.

After he left, she turned away from the gray corner. She stared at the window where the parrot had been.

"I can't try," she told her pillow.

Her pillow never argued. It always accepted her words and absorbed her tears.

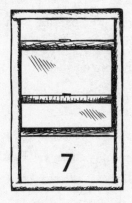

7

A flock swooped past Zeno in a spiral formation toward a nearby roof.

"Great job! Great job! Glad you made it home!"

A man stood next to a little shed. He clapped excitedly as the pigeons fluttered down around him to land on the black tar roof. One pigeon fluttered into his hands. It was all white except for its brown wings. The man gently stroked its back and kissed the top of its head. "Hello, Bunny."

"Brrrooo," Bunny cooed.

Zeno didn't know what to make of this. Of course Dr. Agard stroked him and praised him and called him by name. But Zeno was an African grey parrot. And these birds were—well, there was no polite way to say it—pigeons.

"Everybody okay? Everybody here?" The man counted

twenty-two birds. "I'm so glad you all made it home. Wouldn't want to lose anybody else to a hawk."

The other pigeons were panting with exhaustion. They couldn't even coo.

The man put Bunny down and dumped a big bag of cracked corn into one dish and filled another with water. The pigeons rushed over to eat.

"Okay, darlings, enjoy your dinner. You earned it. One hundred miles in seventy minutes. That's your best time yet. We'll beat Louis Lazar's flock next week for sure."

After the man disappeared through a doorway, Zeno flapped closer to see what was in the dishes. He spread his wings and flashed his scarlet tail to show the pigeons who they had the honor of entertaining. The pigeons didn't step back to demonstrate respect. They didn't even look at Zeno. They kept eating. Their heads bobbled as they pecked at the corn. Bits flew in all directions.

A few landed at Zeno's feet. He picked up a piece with his beak and ate it. It was as hard as a nut, but not nearly as tasty. He walked a few steps closer and picked up another bit of cracked corn. Zeno's beak wasn't shaped for this shameful pecking, but he ate his way over to where the pigeons were crowding around the dish. Zeno hooked his beak over the rim and pulled the dish closer to him.

A black pigeon bumped Zeno with his wing. "Brroo!" it said, which could be translated to mean, *Hey!*

Several more pigeons pushed Zeno away from the dish. Zeno was surprised by this rude behavior, until he remembered that he was dealing with pigeons.

"Zeno want!" he squawked.

He was larger and smarter, of course, but there were so many more of them. They surrounded the dish so that he couldn't even see the cracked corn.

"Mine!" he squawked.

"Broo, brrrooo," the black pigeon said, which meant, *Did you just fly a hundred miles?*

"Hundred?" Zeno squawked. Dr. Agard had encouraged Zeno to count. He had never made it much past seven; however, he did know that one hundred was a very large number.

"Brrrooo, brrrrooo," a gray pigeon said. *You couldn't even fly one.*

Zeno flapped his wings defiantly. Of course he could fly that far. He flapped his wings three more times. Then he folded them against his body. His muscles were a little sore from all the flying he had already done that day. Perhaps these pigeons could fly much farther than he could. He cocked his head. He was still the most beautiful, brilliant bird in Brooklyn, but it might have been possible that he wasn't the best flier.

"Pffft," he muttered, and preened his chest a little. Well, what if he wasn't? He didn't see why anybody would want to fly such a great distance. Zeno wondered if he would fly a hundred miles for a banana-nut muffin. He certainly wouldn't go that far for a dish of cracked corn.

"Zeno doesn't want. Why fly hundred?" Zeno said.

The pigeons bobbled their heads at Zeno and then at each other, as if to say, *Why? Why are you asking why? What do you mean, why?* For they weren't the type of birds who considered the reasons for anything they did.

One pigeon, the white one with the brown wings, looked at Zeno and said, "Brrrrooo," which meant, *to get back home.*

"Home?" Zeno squawked.

Home wasn't one of the 127 words that Zeno knew. He wondered what it meant. He looked at the pigeon, the one the man called Bunny.

"Why?" Zeno squawked again. "Why home?"

Bunny bobbled his head to eat some corn. He rubbed against the black pigeon and the gray pigeon. He drank water. He ate more corn. He rubbed against the black pigeon again. Then he looked at Zeno and said, "Brrooo brroo," which meant, *food friend.*

"Pfft," Zeno muttered. Food? Friend? That didn't make sense. Zeno didn't consider cracked corn to be food. It was more like little rocks. And "friend"? What was "friend"? Bunny must not have known what "home" meant, either.

Then Zeno remembered a story Dr. Agard told about the human Zeno. When someone asked the human Zeno what a friend was, the human Zeno had said, "Another I."

For some reason, Dr. Agard and his assistant had spent hours discussing what this meant. Zeno, however, knew perfectly well that his best friend was himself. So he told the pigeon, "Friend Zeno."

"Brrroo broo," Bunny said. *Friend Zeno.*

"Pfft," Zeno muttered. That wasn't what he meant at all. Bunny wasn't his friend. How could a pigeon possibly be another I? They had the wrong number of toes and garish red feet! Only Zeno could be Zeno. Because, as you know, Zeno was the most beautiful, brilliant bird in Brooklyn.

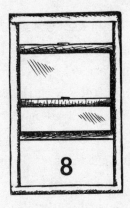

8

Alya sat on the end of the monstrous bed. She held the railing with one hand to steady herself while her mother helped her change out of her sweatpants. Her clothes were too big now. She had to put a safety pin in the waistband of her pants to keep them up. She was getting dressed because she was going out. Yes, she was leaving her bedroom and her house. Where was she going? Someplace fun? Kiki's apartment? A tea shop to meet Liza? The soccer field in Prospect Park? Unfortunately not.

"I can tie my shoes," she said. At least her feet had stayed the same size.

"It's faster if I do it, sweetheart. We don't want to be late." Mrs. Logan quickly made the loops into double knots, just as she had done when Alya was two.

Actually Alya wouldn't have minded being late. She

didn't want to go to the hospital at all. "Is it going to hurt?"

"Oh no," Mrs. Logan said. "It's just an MRI. You had one before, remember? All you have to do is take off your earrings and lie still. That will be easy, won't it?"

Alya sighed. Lying still was all the doctors ever asked her to do. It was what she did best now.

"Are you ready?"

Alya grabbed the plaid cap off the hook her dad had made to keep it by the headboard of her bed. She put the cap firmly on her head and shuffled through the doorway. When she got to the top of the stairs, she paused.

Two flights. Fourteen stairs in each flight. Twenty-eight stairs would be such a long way to fall.

Mrs. Logan watched her closely. "Maybe someone should carry you."

Carry her? Like she was a baby? She was eleven. She didn't need to be carried. She walked down all by herself the last time she had gone to the doctor. That had been two weeks ago.

"Okay," Alya said quietly.

Her mom went to get her brother.

Parker ran up the stairs two at a time. "Need a ride?" He pawed his feet and whinnied like a horse.

"You look more like a donkey to me," Alya said.

"You're the one who's as stubborn as a mule," Parker said.

He boosted Alya up on his back. She squeezed his neck.

"Hey. Stop choking me," Parker said.

"Did you say 'joking me'?" Alya said.

They started down the first flight of stairs.

Mrs. Logan looked up from the landing. "Be careful."

"I'm always careful. I'm the definition of careful. I'm full of care," Parker said.

"Except that time you dropped the watermelon and it rolled off the back porch," Alya said.

"Like this?" Parker dipped his right knee so Alya slid off his right shoulder.

Alya gasped.

"Parker! You'll drop her!" Mrs. Logan screeched.

"Sorry." Parker walked more slowly down the second set of fourteen steps.

Alya sighed. She tried to look over her shoulder, back up the stairs. She couldn't see her room. It was gone. Like so much else.

"How will I get back?" Alya whispered.

"I'll carry you, silly," he said.

That wasn't exactly what she meant. How would she ever get back to the old Alya?

Mr. Logan held the front door open. Mrs. Logan paused at the little table where the mail piled up. She tried to get all the envelopes straight but she couldn't.

"She can't even go down the stairs anymore," Mr. Logan whispered.

"Shhh," Mrs. Logan said. "She'll hear you."

Actually Alya wasn't paying any attention to her parents. As Parker carried her over the threshold, she heard two other voices coming toward her.

"Stop messing with your hair. It looks fine," Kiki said.

"I don't want this curl to stick out. Do you have scissors?" Liza said.

"You're not going to cut it off now. Hurry up or we'll be late."

"Why didn't you tell me what time it was?"

Kiki and Liza ran along the street. They stopped when they saw Alya and her family in a clump right where their stoop met the sidewalk.

"Hi Alya," Kiki called.

"Hi," Liza said.

"Put me down," Alya hissed to Parker.

He did. Her cap fell off. Kiki picked it up. Alya snatched it from her and put it on her head. She clung to the iron fence.

"Where are you going?" Kiki said.

Alya tugged the cap lower over her eyes.

"If it's private, you don't have to say," Liza said.

"Oh, it isn't private. We're taking Alya to have an MRI so the doctor can tell how well the treatment worked," Mrs. Logan said.

"Mo-om," Alya said.

"Your friends want to know," Mrs. Logan said.

Kiki and Liza smiled. Alya didn't.

Why would they want to know? So they could feel sorry for her? So they could tell everybody at school? So that they could all say, no matter how bad the math test was or how horrible the lunch stank or how Lenny bullied kids in gym class, at least we aren't Alya?

"Well," Liza said, as she tucked the stray curl behind her ear.

"It was so nice of you girls to bring that book. I know Alya is so glad to have something fun to read. I loved *The Secret Garden* when I was a girl," Mrs. Logan said.

"Mom, you said we were going to be late," Alya said.

"We have a few minutes," Mrs. Logan said.

"Actually, we better get to school," Kiki said.

"Or we'll be late," Liza said.

"Bye, Alya." The girls tried to hug her but Alya kept one hand on her cap and the other hand on the iron fence.

"I'm sure the doctor will have something good to say," Kiki said.

"Oh, yeah," Alya said. Doctors always did—even it was only how brave she was to let them stick her with needles.

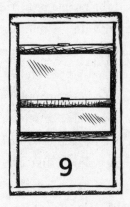

9

The cracked corn only made Zeno hungrier. The pigeons may have been content to peck at those hard bits, but Zeno was not a pigeon. He flew off to search for food more suited to one such as him—in other words, banana-nut muffins.

Dr. Agard always encouraged Zeno to follow where reason led, just as the human Zeno advised. Now, you probably know that reason can lead to different places. However, Zeno focused on just a few facts. Dr. Agard always brought the muffins in a bag. The human who wasn't Dr. Agard had also carried food in a bag. The dark brown circle with the colored dots wasn't the food Zeno wanted. So that meant Zeno just had to find the right bag.

"Banana nut. Follow reason. Booful, briyant bird," Zeno squawked.

He was quite pleased with himself as he perched on a branch and watched the people pass. He thought it would be easy to find the bag with the muffins, until he saw how many bags there were. Almost every human, no matter what its shape or size, carried a bag. Many carried more than one. How would Zeno ever figure out which bag contained muffins? The bags were also different shapes and sizes. Some were black, like the material of Dr. Agard's shoes. Others were brightly colored, like Dr. Agard's pajamas. One small human even had a bag that was shaped like a parrot. Was this a tribute? Or was this why Zeno never saw other parrots?

"Pfft," he muttered, and flew to a higher branch. Did he despair? Of course not. He was Zeno. Hadn't he learned how to say 127 words? If he watched these humans long enough, he was confident that he could follow where their reason led—straight to a banana-nut muffin.

So he kept watching. He didn't preen, as tempting as it was to give his chest feathers a little stroke. He raised his right foot to point at the sidewalk below and observed.

At first he focused his attention on the largest bags. Well, why not? Zeno understood the concept of "more." Reason led him to think that the largest bags would have the most muffins. Humans carried these black shiny bags out of their houses, dropped them in cans in their front yards, and quickly walked away. Zeno considered ripping one open with his beak. However, he decided that if humans didn't want what was in them, he wouldn't, either.

Humans carried smaller, square bags close to their bodies. Reason led Zeno to think that humans valued what was in these bags. What could it be, he wondered? Then he saw a human reach into hers and take out that small black rectangle that humans liked to talk to.

"Hello?" the human said. "Oh, hi, how are you?"

"Pfft," Zeno muttered. If he wanted to have an intelligent conversation, he talked to himself—not to a contraption.

A large dog led a human along the sidewalk. The human was tied to the dog with a long red rope.

Zeno was sorry he hadn't kept Dr. Agard tied up. Then maybe his servant wouldn't have been taken away from him.

The human carried a small blue bag. It seemed empty, so Zeno didn't pay much attention to it. The dog stopped right under the tree where Zeno was perched. The dog squatted down and did his business. Then the human leaned over, put the poop inside the blue bag, and carried that bag down the street.

Zeno was horrified. He flapped away in the opposite direction. He abandoned his idea of observing bags. He couldn't trust humans ever again. There was no telling what they carried with them. Reason hadn't led him very far. How could it, when humans weren't reasonable?

He flew up over a rooftop, down along another street. And there he saw the very thing he had been seeking. A white plastic bag with blue markings was hanging from the branch of a tree.

"Nuts," he squawked. Now it was obvious. Muffins didn't grow on trees. *Bags* of muffins did.

Zeno flapped over to the tree. The bag was tangled in the small branches. Zeno plucked at the handle and tried to yank it loose. It wasn't easy. As soon as he freed it from one branch, it got twisted up with another. He clung to the branch with his feet as he stuck his head inside the bag to pull out the muffin. Before he quite understood what had happened, he was hopelessly tangled.

"Brawwk!" he squawked.

Being upside down and somewhat inside out wasn't very comfortable. To make matters worse, with his head in the bag, he could see that it didn't contain banana-nut muffins. In fact, it didn't contain anything edible at all—just one of those sticks Dr. Agard used to mark on paper. The stick fell to the ground, but Zeno was still stuck.

"Brrroo?" which meant, *Are you okay?*

"Crawp crawp crawp," Zeno squawked, which needed no translation.

The other bird grabbed the edge of the plastic bag with its beak and pulled it away from Zeno's face.

"Brrroo!" which meant, *I know you.*

The other bird was Bunny.

As Bunny held the bag, Zeno was able to tear the plastic. After tugging this way and that, Zeno ripped the handle. The plastic fell down from the branch. The two birds blinked at each other for a moment. They were both glad that Zeno was free.

"Brroo," said Bunny. *I guess I'll go home now.*

"Brawk?" squawked Zeno. He still wasn't sure what "home" meant. However, he remembered the cracked corn. After spending all that time studying the humans, he hadn't found anything else he could eat.

"Brroo?" said Bunny. *Would you like to come?*

Zeno opened his beak. He was hungry. Reason should have led him to that food. But Zeno got distracted by two other pigeons who fluttered down to the sidewalk below.

These pigeons bobbled their heads as they walked. Didn't they know how ridiculous they looked pitter-pattering on their little red feet? *Brroo, brroo, brroo.* Didn't they have any pride? They could have at least tried to walk properly like a parrot. *Brroo, brroo, brroo.* Now they were rubbing against each other in a very sloppy way.

Zeno stared at Bunny.

"Brroo?" Bunny said. *Are you coming?*

"Pfft," Zeno muttered. He knew he was hungry, but he also knew he wasn't a pigeon.

Then he heard a loud "Brak!"

He saw a flash of green as another bird flew over his head. It was a parrot.

So Zeno, without saying another word to Bunny, followed where that parrot led.

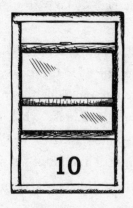

10

"Hello? Hello?" Zeno squawked as he followed the bright green parrot with the round head. He was very excited to talk with his cousin. A parrot could show him where to find parrot food and a parrot place to live—and most important, appreciate Zeno's parrot gifts. "Zeno, Zeno. Booful briyant Zeno!"

The green parrot didn't seem to hear Zeno. He joined a flock of other Monk parrots who had been eating pinecones.

When Zeno saw thirty birds flying back to their colony, he whistled. Maybe you're shocked, too, that so many wild parrots live in Brooklyn, of all places. But that really is true. Hundreds and hundreds of Monk parrots have nested in Brooklyn for more than forty years, ever since an event they call the "Great Escape." You'll hear more about it later. At this moment, Zeno was trying to catch up to his cousins. "Hello hello? Zeno here. Zeno parrot. You parrot. Parrot good."

The Monks paid no attention whatsoever to the African grey parrot. They chattered to themselves as they flew over the roofs of the houses and along the tree-lined streets of Brooklyn. "Brak brak brak brak," which meant, *Everybody here? Hurry up. You fly too fast. Well, you fly too slow.*

Soon they arrived at a forest of tall metal frames connected by thick cables. Many years ago, the Monks had discovered that this was a perfect place to make their nests. The frames were always warm, even in the winter. And best of all, humans didn't dare come too close. The power that buzzed through the wires was both feared by humans—and adored. It made music, computers, ice cream, and all good things possible.

Zeno knew nothing about the advantages of electricity. He had noticed another spot. Just across the street from the buzzing nests was the grand entrance to Green-Wood Cemetery. High above the arch was an ornate brown spire.

"Kathekon!" Zeno cried as he flew toward it. Kathekon was one of the human Zeno's Greek words. It could be translated to mean *in agreement with nature*. In other words, what could be more fitting than that the most beautiful, brilliant bird in Brooklyn perch on top of that exquisite spire so he could look down on everyone. At least, that was what Zeno thought.

And so he flew directly to it and clung to the brown stone with his long toes.

"Kathekon booful briyant Zeno!" he cried.

"Brak," squawked one of the Monk parrots right below Zeno's feet.

Zeno looked down. Several small nests were tucked among the decorative carvings. So Zeno repeated himself. "Kathekon booful briyant Zeno!" He spoke more slowly and loudly because even though these were parrots, he didn't know how many words they understood.

The answer to that was none. No human had ever spoken to them before. None of them had ever been owned—not by a breeder, a scientist, a professor, or even a pirate.

"Brak brak brak brak," they chattered among themselves. *What is that big ugly gray thing doing here?*

"Brak brak brak," squawked one Monk. *He's got no right to be on top.*

This was Vack. The sapphire tips of his wings were just a bit brighter than the other Monks. He worked just a bit harder to advance his position within the flock. He had been planning for years how to occupy the top.

Of course, Zeno didn't know about their complex power struggles. And even if he did, he wouldn't have cared about their pecking order. He wasn't part of their flock.

"Brak brak brak," Vack shouted. *You can't sit on the spire.*

Zeno flapped his wings and flashed his tail. He thought he needed no introduction. However, he was happy to provide one. "Zeno want stay. Kathekon! Zeno speak words, not brak brak brak."

"Brak," Vack squawked. *So?*

So? Zeno blinked. Why weren't these parrots amazed by this accomplishment?

"Human words!" Zeno squawked again.

Vack flew up to grab hold of the spire right next to Zeno. He was so close that Zeno could see the battle scars on Vack's orange snub beak. "Brak brak brak," Vack squawked. *We hate humans.*

"Brak?" Zeno squawked. *Why?*

Then all the Monks chattered. "Brak brak brak brak brak." For they all knew the story. From the moment they cracked out of their eggs, their parents told them how their ancestors had lived in paradise. Until humans had trapped the parrots and brought them to this country imprisoned in wooden crates. Many birds had died in this terrible crossing. Only the bravest had survived. They were determined to escape to a better life. They waited in the dark crates for the right moment. When a human pried off the lid, the brave birds burst forth. They attacked the humans with their claws and their beaks. The humans fell backward in defeat.

That was the Great Escape.

"Pfft," Zeno muttered. The story had impressed him a little. However, he didn't see what it had to do with him. He had never been in a crate—or even a cage. He had seen cages, of course. Dr. Agard used to store his important papers in a wire box to keep Zeno from gnawing them.

Then Vack said, "Brak brak brak," which meant, *Humans and their traitors are not welcome here.* He flew at Zeno and scraped him with one sapphire-tipped wing.

"Brawk!" Zeno squawked. He never expected to be challenged. Certainly not by one of his cousins.

"Brak brak brak." The other Monks screeched something that meant (in more polite terms), *Let's put this arrogant gray intruder in his place.*

"Crawp green parrots!" Zeno squawked. It was the worst insult he knew.

The Monks sure understood that. Vack swooped at Zeno again and sounded an alarm call about him. "Brak brak brak brak!"

"Brak brak brak brak brak!" More and more Monks came from as far away as the buzzing nests to join the attack.

Zeno clung to his perch with one foot and tried to defend himself with the other.

"Booful, briyant Zeno," he squawked.

His boasting only made the Monks angrier. Again and again they attacked.

Zeno didn't want to abandon his perch. Why, if he let those round-headed Monks push him away, he wouldn't be the most beautiful, brilliant bird in Brooklyn. And yet, as the attack continued, he was in danger of losing more than his self-respect.

Then, as he twisted his head to avoid Vack's claws, he noticed another tall stone column beyond a small pool of water. This column was not nearly as ornate; however, it was topped with a statue of something with wings. Zeno decided to fly over to see what it was. He wasn't retreating. Oh no, he could have continued to battle his cousins until they admitted his superiority. He just didn't want to hurt them.

Zeno perched on the top of what turned out to be a man's head. A man with wings? What could that be?

"Parrot man?" Zeno muttered. He rubbed his beak against the Parrot Man's wings. The stone was rough and comforting. He was quite pleased with his spot. He spread his own wings in just the same way as the Parrot Man. He was sure that he looked quite handsome in that pose. He had no doubt that the Monks would soon be clamoring to pay him the attention he deserved.

In fact, while Zeno preened, Vack and several Monks zipped past, as if drawing a line in the sky that Zeno should not cross.

"Brak brak," Vack cried. *We defeated humans in the Great Escape.*

"Brak brak brak," the other Monks chattered. *And now we taught this gray know-it-all who's boss.*

"Kathekon Zeno Parrot Man!" Zeno squawked. He

flapped his wings three times to show the Monk parrots he didn't care about them or their ancestors. He didn't need anybody. His perch was a far better place than the brown spire.

The Parrot Man didn't argue with him or chase him. The Parrot Man adored him. He allowed Zeno to rub his beak against his stone wings. Zeno didn't need any more proof of devotion than that. Except it would have been nice if the Parrot Man brought him a banana-nut muffin. Or if the Parrot Man told Zeno what a beautiful, brilliant bird he was. Or called him by name.

No one had properly spoken to Zeno since Dr. Agard had left. To be accurate, Bunny had called him a friend— but Bunny was a pigeon. The girl in the bed had talked to Zeno—but she hadn't praised him. She had been too busy thinking about herself. Why, she had actually refused to give him the muffin.

Zeno rubbed against the Parrot Man's rough wing again.

"Booful briyant Zeno?" he muttered.

The Parrot Man didn't disagree—or agree. He was as silent as, well, a stone.

11

*B*rring *brring brrring.* The loud ringing sounded like an alarm, as if the house were under attack.

"I'll get it," Mrs. Logan called from downstairs.

Alya certainly wasn't going to run to answer the phone. She knew the only people who ever called that number were telemarketers—and her doctor.

"Oh, hello, Dr. Jones," Mrs. Logan said cheerfully. "Do you have the test results?"

Alya sat up. She held her breath. Hoping to hear. Hoping not to hear. She gripped the railing. It felt like the monkey bars. Please, she thought, don't let me fall again.

"Hold on just a minute."

Downstairs, a door shut and Alya couldn't hear her mom's voice anymore.

Alya waited. And waited. How long could it take to say what the MRI had found?

She tried to keep her eyes on the blue sky part of the wall. She really tried. She turned her head away from the gray corner. Why shouldn't she have good news this time? Hadn't she had the awful treatments? She had. The treatments must have worked. They had taken away her hair.

But as her mom continued to talk to Dr. Jones, Alya's eyes slid back to the dark corner. It was bigger. Late in the afternoon, the shadow of her dresser contaminated the blue.

Then there were footsteps on the stairs. Slow steps. Was her mom dreading the moment she would enter the room?

The door swung open. Mrs. Logan carried a tray with a glass of pink liquid that was supposed to be full of energy boosters. She carefully put the tray down on the table by the window and hugged Alya over the railing.

"What?" Alya said.

"I was just on the phone with Dr. Jones. She said your MRI looked really good."

"It did?" Alya couldn't believe it. "Really?"

"Really. That's such great news."

Mrs. Logan hugged Alya again, for a longer time, and kept her face hidden from Alya until the danger of tears had passed.

"Yes. Such great news. Now take a big drink of this." Mrs. Logan pushed the button to make the top of the bed rise up. She put the straw close to Alya's lips. Alya took a little sip.

"That's my girl. How about another sip?"

Alya shook her head.

"Are you sure you can't manage just a little bit more? It's really good for you."

Alya wrinkled her nose and shook her head. "I don't need it now. Do I?"

Mrs. Logan sighed and put the glass down on the table. She pulled the chair close to the bed and stuck her arm through the railing to hold Alya's hand.

"What?" Alya said.

"Dr. Jones says you're ready to start the second phase of chemo next Tuesday." Mrs. Logan tried to sound like this was a good thing.

"The second phase?"

"They want to make sure they got it all." Mrs. Logan smiled and squeezed Alya's hand.

Alya lay back against the pillow. The fabric rubbed her tiny hairs the wrong way. They had just started to grow. They shouldn't have bothered. They were only going to fall out anyway. What was the point when the doctors would always say that Alya needed more and more treatments? What was the point of anything when everybody everywhere in the whole wide world was eventually going to die?

"It won't be so bad. Really. You did fine before. You're so brave. You never make a fuss about anything."

No, Alya thought. She just lay there while they did whatever they needed to do.

"There's only one problem. And it isn't exactly a problem, it's just a little thing we have to deal with. But we'll figure out something, so don't you worry."

"What?" Alya said.

Mrs. Logan got very busy smoothing blankets and adjusting the pillow as she spoke in a great rush. "Now, the first treatment on Tuesday won't be so bad. Parker can stay home from school to help you get up and down the stairs that day, unless he has a test of course, but he probably doesn't. And maybe your dad could manage, even though he has a bad back, because you hardly weigh a thing. But you have to go so many times for all those weeks. Back and forth and up and down the stairs, and I just don't see how in the world we're ever going to get you up and down and back and forth and . . ."

Alya heard the panic taint her mom's voice, like the dark spreading out from the corner that should have been blue.

"I'm sorry," Alya said.

"Oh, honey, no, you have nothing to be sorry about. Nothing. I'm sorry. I shouldn't have said all that." Mrs. Logan hugged Alya and stroked the top of her forehead for the 9,595th time. "We'll work it out. In fact, I'll call your dad right now. I'm sure he'll have a good idea. You know him and his ideas. Besides, he'll be so happy to hear the good news, right?"

Alya sighed. Would she ever have good news that wasn't bad?

"Now don't you worry. Just rest. I'll lower the bed." Mrs. Logan pushed the button. The bed went back down. She lowered the rail so she could tuck the covers in tight. Alya stared at her legs as her mother snapped the railing back into place. It clanged like a prison cell door.

"Mom? Why can't I walk anymore?" Alya said.

Mrs. Logan frowned. She had never been very good at answering her children's "why" questions. Why was the sky blue? Why did a ball bounce? Why did some of Alya's cells run amok when Mrs. Logan's own cells did what they were supposed to do? Mrs. Logan tried her best to explain. "Well, you know the leukemia made you tired. And now I guess maybe you've spent so much time resting in bed, your muscles have gotten weak."

Alya thought about this. "So I could walk better, if I tried?"

"Yes. Well, I don't actually know. Maybe." Mrs. Logan didn't sound very sure. "I mean, we wouldn't want you to fall. You bruise so easily. I'll ask Dr. Jones, the very next time she calls. Okay?"

"I want to walk more."

"Of course you do, sweetheart. And you will walk more.

You will." Mrs. Logan stroked Alya's forehead for the 9,596th time. "I'll be back in a little bit. Don't worry. I'm sure we'll find some way to keep you from having to stay at the hospital."

Mrs. Logan tiptoed out of the room and quietly shut the door behind her.

She might just as well have slammed it. The floor, the walls, the bed all shuddered as if there were an earthquake. Gray dust settled all over the blue.

That might very well have been the end of hope except that outside the window, a bird squawked.

Alya quickly turned to see who it was. It was just a blue jay. The parrot hadn't come back. She felt so disappointed. She hadn't known how much she wanted to see Zeno until he wasn't there.

"Go away. I don't want you," Alya said.

The jay squawked again, as if to say, *Why not?*

"Because I want Zeno. The African grey parrot."

The jay squawked again, as if to say, *Why?*

She couldn't explain to a bird what she didn't really understand herself. She took a deep breath and asked more politely. "If, by chance, you see Zeno, would you please tell him that Alya needs him?"

The blue jay squawked and flew away.

Alya felt very silly. She was glad Parker hadn't heard her talking to a bird. He would have teased her mercilessly. He would have said she belonged in a mental hospital. Not the kind with sick children where she was going to have to go next Tuesday because her body had betrayed her and she couldn't climb two-and-a-half flights of stairs.

The message quickly spread. The blue jay told a pigeon marching along the sidewalk. The pigeon told a sparrow who told a mourning dove who told a cardinal. And so forth and so on. Each time a bird heard the message, it shook its head and said, "Too bad she needs a parrot."

The birds all knew that parrots thought they were better than other animals just because they could speak human *and* bird. Parrots never helped anybody.

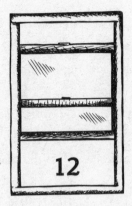

12

Zeno swallowed his pride and ate beetles. He slept out-side in the rain. These indignities were only temporary. Eventually the Monk parrots would treat him with more respect and share their food and shelter. In the meantime, he worked on his feathers. It was hard to be beautiful when the wind was always ruffling them.

A raucous burst of chatter from the Monk parrots dis-turbed his preening. As days passed, he no longer paid any attention to what they were saying. He was tired of hearing about the Great Escape. Or what clever things their babies had done. Why should Zeno care who was flapping and ready to learn to fly?

Then Vack and a few other Monk parrots flew to a tree near the Parrot Man.

"Brak brak brak," Vack said, which meant, *There he is, the silly gray thing.*

Then all the Monks chattered, "Brak brak brak!" *Ha ha ha, did you ever hear anything so ridiculous in your whole life?*

Were the Monks laughing—at him? "Brawwwk!" Zeno squawked. *What's so funny?*

"Brak brak brak!" Vack said, which meant, *A girl needs a gray parrot.*

"Pfft," Zeno muttered. What did that have to do with him?

The other Monks laughed and laughed. "Brak brak brak brak." *You better go be with humans and stop hanging around here.*

"Brawk," Zeno squawked. There must be other gray parrots. Why, even the Parrot Man was gray.

"Brak brak brak," Vack said. *The cardinal said the girl said Zeno.*

Zeno? He turned his head upside down. What girl knew his name? He didn't know any girls. Then he remembered talking with the girl in the large bed. She had liked his name. She had been impressed by his ability to speak. It had to be her.

Of course the girl wanted Zeno. Who wouldn't want a brilliant bird with a beautiful scarlet tail? He displayed it for the Monk parrots. They were only green—a color as common as grass.

"Brak brak brak." The Monk parrots kept laughing and chattering among themselves.

"Zeno want!" Zeno squawked. He didn't know the word for respect. He doubted whether the Monks could ever treat him the way he deserved. Clearly they were too ignorant to appreciate a bird of his caliber. Maybe he should go see the girl. Yes yes yes, he bobbed up and down excitedly. Obviously the girl had come to her senses and decided to give him the banana-nut muffin.

Oh, Zeno. Were the other birds right about parrots? It was true that many parrots knew how to talk. A few could identify colors and shapes. Some had even been taught to ride little bicycles in the circus. Could they ever learn to care about anything that didn't look exactly like themselves?

"Banana nut!" Zeno squawked. He flapped his wings and soared into the sky.

"Brak brak," Vack said. *Go be her pet.*

"Brawk!" How dare Vack call Zeno a pet! Zeno was so angry, he circled back to fight. He could have easily defeated that snub-beak Vack. And his round-headed friends. All thirty of them. Plus the forty who lived over in the buzzing nests. But Zeno hadn't had much breakfast. He decided it was more important to get that muffin.

He flew along a quiet street back toward where the girl lived. Well, toward where he *thought* the girl lived. He passed many buildings and multiple trees, some of which actually were the same tree. He mistakenly believed that they looked familiar because, as everyone knows, all trees look alike. He refused to admit the small possibility that he didn't know where he was going. Of course he knew. Wasn't he Zeno?

The flying made him tired. He perched on top of an iron fence and rubbed his beak alongside an ornate spike.

He thought of Bunny and the pigeons who flew a hundred miles. He wondered how they always found their way to that place Bunny had called home, whatever that was. Of course, Zeno wasn't looking for home. He was in search of a girl with a muffin. Why hadn't the cardinal told Vack where the girl lived?

"Pffft," Zeno muttered.

Vack probably couldn't have said the rest of the message. Vack wasn't as smart as Zeno.

"Banana nut," Zeno muttered encouragingly to himself. Then he said it a little louder. "Banana banana nut nut."

Yes, the muffin was there waiting for him. He would find it. He would.

"Zeno wants!" And, moreover, a bird like Zeno deserved to get what he wanted. Wasn't that how things should be? Wasn't that what the human Zeno meant by Kathekon? "Kathekon Zeno muffin!" He flapped his wings proudly and showed the scarlet of his tail.

This exciting display of feathers caught the attention of

a human who was walking along the opposite side of the street.

Zeno paid no attention to the way that man stared at him. He didn't see the man crouch down behind a parked car and reach into his shoulder bag. The man held a crumpled object in both hands as he crept across the street. Unfortunately, Zeno wasn't curious about the absurd behavior of humans. As usual, Zeno was only thinking about himself.

He had to get help, no, not help—assistance—without exactly asking for it. He had trained Dr. Agard to believe that being Zeno's servant was a great honor. Zeno just needed to inform a few chosen birds that he had decided to bestow a similar privilege upon them. He was going to allow them to guide him to the girl and her banana-nut muffin. Just like when Bunny had paid Zeno the tribute of removing the plastic bag.

"Zeno want!" he squawked.

A flock of brown sparrows were loitering in a nearby tree. Zeno would have preferred to be escorted by the cardinal. Its red feathers would have complemented the scarlet in Zeno's tail. However, Zeno was too hungry to delay getting his muffin. Sparrows would have to do.

"Zeno. Girl," Zeno squawked.

"Bre bre bre bre bre bre bre." The sparrows chattered excitedly to one another.

"Zeno girl banana nut!" Zeno squawked louder.

The sparrows instantly got quiet.

Ah, Zeno was delighted that his plan was working perfectly.

Then the sparrows scattered.

Zeno was stunned. How could they be so rude? Obviously they hadn't understood what he wanted. They were just common sparrows, after all, with a limited vocabulary.

He comforted himself by turning his head upside down and rubbing his beautiful beak along the rough stones of the wall. He would just have to find other birds. Better birds. Birds who would appreciate the opportunity to serve Zeno. Those sparrows would be sorry they had flown away.

Or so he thought.

Then, on the ground below him, he noticed two bright white shoes tied with long, orange laces. Dr. Agard never had shoes like that. His shoes had been brown with a flap that stuck up conveniently for Zeno to chew. He wondered if these orange laces would be nice to gnaw. Some things were and some things weren't. Stiffness was important, but so was texture. Really the only test was to grab hold of the object with his beak. He opened his mouth and slowly leaned closer. He was so focused on those laces that he didn't see the big black bag—until he was trapped inside it.

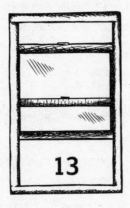

13

Alya floated in her bed on waves of downstairs voices. She heard her mom's shrill panic. "You can't carry her every day. You'll throw your back out again. Then where will we be?" She heard her dad's fuzzy optimism. "Maybe if I rig up some kind of pulley?" She heard Parker slamming something, not a door, maybe his hand against the table? "*I* will carry her. I told you that already."

"You have school," Alya said even though no one could hear her. High school was hard, even for Parker. She didn't want him to get behind. She wanted him to play sports and be with his friends and do everything that she couldn't do anymore.

Downstairs the front door banged shut. Her family had gone. That was fine. She didn't need to know where they went or when they would be back. She was glad they left.

She didn't want them hanging around feeling sorry that she was stuck up here. Why would she need them to keep her company when she had a monster who lived in the gray corner of the room?

"You better find somebody new to terrorize. I might be leaving soon."

She quickly turned away. She didn't think that she should let a monster see her cry.

When she rolled toward her right, she felt a sharp stabbing pain in her side. She froze.

She had had pains before. You may not realize it, but lying in bed isn't very comfortable after the first day or so. She always had aching joints and a stiff neck and that terrible tenderness in her belly.

This was different. This was a sharp pain. Stabbing her somewhere near one of those parts of her body that probably was extremely crucial even though she never paid any attention to it before things started to fall apart.

The pain wasn't going away.

Was it her spleen? What was the spleen? Who ever even heard of the spleen? Dr. Jones had. She knew all kinds of things that Alya didn't. She had known Alya needed more treatment. Dr. Jones had known that the cancer cells might be hiding someplace the MRI couldn't see. And she had been right. Only now it was too late to poison the cells to death. They were multiplying and multiplying inside

Alya's spleen. Before too long, there would be so many, her spleen would burst.

"Nooooo!" she screamed.

Parker came running. "What's wrong?"

He walked around the bed and squatted down so that his face was level with hers. He clung to the railing. "What is it?"

"It hurts," she whispered.

"I'll call Mom and Dad. They just went to the store."

Alya shook her head. "It's too late."

"What are you talking about? Of course it's not too late."

"My spleen is full."

"You want me to help you to the bathroom?" He would do that for his sister, as weird as it would be.

"Of cancer. That's why it hurts."

"Oh." Parker didn't know what to do. "I better call Mom and Dad. Just lie back. You're all scrunched up. Here. Let me help you get comfortable."

He slid his hand under her hip to ease her back to the middle of the bed. Then he felt something, too. "Um, Alya?"

Parker pulled his hand out from under her. He closed his fist and hid it behind him. "How do you feel now?"

Alya waited for signals from outposts all over her body. Toes, fingers, hips, spleen. All reported calm. "I don't notice it so much anymore. Oh, Parker. Maybe the cancer damaged my nerves. Maybe that's why I can't feel anything. It could spread anywhere, you know. Anywhere blood goes, and blood goes everywhere."

With a flourish, Parker brought his hand forward and opened his fist to reveal a large safety pin. It was bent so much that its sharp point was unsheathed.

Alya stared at it. It was the pin she used to keep her pants up. "Where did you get that?"

"It was sticking into your side."

Alya rolled over and looked at the waist band of her sweatpants. The pin was gone. She lifted her shirt and saw an angry red mark where the pin had stabbed her. She pulled down her shirt and lay back on the bed. "Oh."

"Oh?" Parker burst out laughing.

"It isn't funny." Alya folded her arms across her chest.

"Yes it is." Parker taunted her with the pin.

"I thought I was dying!"

Parker put the pin on top of her dresser. He couldn't face her, so he let his head hang down between his arms as he mumbled, "I'm sorry."

Alya was sorry, too. It wasn't his fault. She sat up. More than anything she wanted to run over and jump on his back or punch him in the arm. If only it weren't such a long way to go. Finally she said, "Hey, Parker. You cured me."

He wiped his face on his arm and smiled at her. "That's right. I did."

"You can be my doctor now. I'll fire Dr. Jones. She's too cautious."

"Well, she is a grown-up."

"That's right. From now on, whenever I need curing, you can just take a safety pin out of my bed. No more treatments for me."

Alya took her plaid cap off its special hook and threw it across the room. It landed right at the mouth of the gray corner.

Parker went to pick it up. "Gee. Nobody finished painting your room."

"I know."

"We got to do that."

"Mom's afraid the fumes will make me nauseous."

"Doesn't it drive you crazy to have it like that? I know what we can do." Parker shoved the dresser toward the gray corner.

"You can't cover it up. I know it's there. I'll always know it's there."

Parker stopped. Then he pushed the dresser back. "Well, one thing's for sure. I'm going to be carrying you up and down the stairs, so you won't have to stay at the hospital."

"What about school? You can't miss school."

"If you can stay home, I can, too. It's only fair." Parker spoke vehemently, but they both knew that there was no such thing as fair.

They heard the front door bang open.

"Parker? Come help bring in the groceries," their dad called up the stairs.

"Coming," Parker shouted. He pointed his finger at his sister. "See you later."

"I'll be here." Alya did her best to make it sound like a joke. And not like she would be waiting and worrying, and worrying and waiting.

"I'll send you a bill. For curing you and everything," Parker said.

Alya smiled. "Ha, ha."

He was practically out the door when she said, "Parker? I was wondering if maybe you'd seen a bird."

"Sure. Lots. Every day that old guy tosses out bread for the pigeons."

"Have you seen Zeno? The parrot who was here?"

"The African grey? No, I haven't."

"Oh." Alya let her hand fall off the railing.

"What do you want a parrot for? I could understand a cat maybe. Something furry and cute. Or a dog, to bring you things that fall on the floor. But what good is a parrot?"

"I need him to teach me to try. I forgot how, I think."

"What do you mean, you forgot how?" Parker's voice cracked unexpectedly. This happened sometimes. He was on the border between being a boy and a man. Unfortunately, those moments when he most wanted to be a man were when he broke back into being a boy.

"I don't know how it happened. I was concentrating on being a good patient. Like everybody wanted. So I stopped trying. I didn't even realize it until Zeno told me to. That's why I need him to help me."

Parker nodded. He came back to reach over the railing and give her a solemn handshake. "Okay, then. He'll be here. I promise."

"How do you know?" Alya looked into his brown eyes. She badly wanted to believe him.

"Because I'm going to go find him."

14

It was dark inside the bag and difficult to breathe. Zeno couldn't turn right-side up. His left wing was twisted in a painful way. He kept trying to fly and trying to stand up and trying to bite. Only he couldn't do any of those things. He couldn't even squawk properly.

"Brrrp," he mumbled. That wasn't a sound any self-respecting parrot would make, so he didn't do it again.

He was very frightened. He knew he was being taken somewhere—but where? And why?

Fear paralyzed the part of his brain where he kept his human words. That was a problem. Clearly it was a human who had captured him. Only a human wore shoes. Only a human was capable of an atrocity like this. If Zeno could only find the right words, the human might be persuaded to open the bag and let Zeno go. Maybe if Zeno said, "My dear fellow, would you care to reconsider the wisdom of putting a parrot in a black bag?"

Actually a good strong cry of "Help!" would have done the trick.

Alas, "help" was not one of Zeno's 127 words. Why had Dr. Agard taught Zeno to say things like "kathekon"? What good was that?

The bag bounced with each step the human took. Again and again, Zeno bumped against the human's back. Zeno kept trying to wriggle into a better position. Finally, after a great deal of struggle, he managed to tuck his left wing against his body in the proper fashion.

"Good bird," he muttered. Dr. Agard always said that whenever Zeno did something impressive, like quoting the human Zeno. Those accomplishments were small. Now Zeno was being put to a greater challenge. He had to escape from this horrifying, humiliating situation. But how could he get out of the bag?

The Monk parrots always bragged about how their ancestors had escaped from their crate. Well, if green round-headed birds could, so could Zeno.

The human stopped walking. Zeno heard a sound he recognized—a key inserted in a lock. A door opened. The human kept moving. The door shut. *Bang.*

Zeno knew he was in a building. But what kind? There was an overpowering smell of other animals. The stench was so strong that Zeno couldn't identify the separate components. He heard loud chattering. Birds? Frightened birds?

Zeno had never heard sounds like these.

The chattering increased. Birds begging for food and water. Birds quarreling with other birds. Birds desperately crying out for help.

The bag swung. Zeno lost his balance. He was on his back again. He struggled to turn himself over. It was very difficult because there was nothing hard to push off against. He tried to use his wings. If only he could flap them in his enemy's face. If only he could flash his scarlet tail and terrify the human. If only he could get a good chomp of the human's hand. The human swung the bag again. Zeno hit a hard surface. A metal door clanged shut. The human poked Zeno with a stick and somehow dragged away the bag.

Zeno was so happy to be free. He spread his wings. His feathers banged against metal bars.

He was in a cage.

"Brawwwk!" Zeno squawked. He used his beak to pull himself up along the bars. The bottom of the cage was littered with bits of seed and dried poop. That was an outrage. He had never been so angry. He flapped his wings furiously even though it hurt when they banged against the bars. "BRAWWK!"

The other birds chattered and screeched.

What kind of a place was this? The room was so dimly lit, Zeno could barely see.

The human peered at him. He was a male, like Dr. Agard, but much younger. He didn't have glass circles in front of his eyes. He wore a black cap with the bill in the back. "You sure are big for a parrot," the human said.

Big? Why did he say big? Was he going to eat Zeno?

"BRAWWWWK!" Zeno cried.

The other birds in the room were smaller. Small song birds and little parrots, smaller than the Monks. The bright blues and greens and yellows glowed in the shadows.

"Too bad you're gray. Most people like those pretty colors."

"Pfffft." Zeno tried to move away. The cage was so cramped, it was difficult to turn around. Finally, after several tries, he succeeded. Then he was sorry he had.

Coming from the far corner of the room, he could just barely hear plaintive little peeps. Babies? Yes, there were babies. Crying to be fed.

The human was leaving the room. When he opened a door, a shaft of light split the gloom and showed the little ones with their mouths opened wide, waiting for parents who would never come.

How could that human walk away like that? He must have heard the babies. How could he ignore them? The door was shutting. The light was shrinking.

"Feed them!" Zeno squawked.

The human stopped. He called to someone in the other room. "Hey, this guy talks."

"Feed them!" Zeno squawked.

The human turned on a light and came closer. He had listened to Zeno. He was going to feed those poor little babies.

"Feed them!" Zeno squawked. He wasn't sure what babies ate. He didn't think he should request banana-nut muffins for them. Muffins were Zeno's special treat. So instead he squawked, "Nuts nuts nuts!"

The human didn't go help the babies. He came to Zeno's cage and said, "Polly want a cracker?"

What was wrong with these humans? "Brawwwk!" Zeno squawked again. No human word could express his frustration.

Then another man came into the room. He was older. He did have the glass circles in front of his eyes and not very much hair on top of his head. Perhaps not very much of anything in his head, either, because when he came over to Zeno, he also said, "Polly want a cracker?"

"Pffft." Zeno turned his back and moved as far away as he could—six whole inches to the far side of the cage.

"Polly want a cookie? Polly want a cheeseburger? Polly want a chicken-salad sandwich?"

Zeno narrowed his eyes to glare at the old man.

"Polly want a kick in the pants?"

The men watched Zeno for nearly a minute. The old man shook his head. "I don't hear nothing."

"Come on, Polly." The young man clanked his thick ring against the side of the cage.

"When we say they talk, they got to talk," the old man said.

"Maybe it's got nothing to say," the young man said.

Zeno had plenty to say. To begin with, what was the idea of kidnapping him and putting him in this horrible cage? But more important, what about those poor babies?

"Feed them! Nuts nuts nuts!" Zeno squawked.

The old man pounded the young man on the back. "It does talk! Way to go, Slim. You did good to bring him in. Yessir. You can talk, can't you? Smart bird, aren't you?"

The old man reached in his pocket and took out a piece of food. He offered it to Zeno.

"Feed *them*." Zeno muttered. But he ate the pellet.

"Can't have a smart bird like you stuck back here, can we? Come on. Help me with this."

The old man grabbed one side of the cage. The man called Slim lifted the other.

"Zeno Zeno Zeno!" Zeno squawked triumphantly.

They carried him out of the dark room and away from the starving babies. Now that the men knew who he was, they were certain to set him free.

Or so Zeno thought.

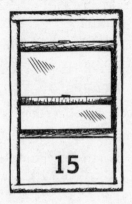

15

The men carried Zeno's cage into a room with a door that would lead to the street, the trees, the birds flying up into the sky. "Zeno want!" he squawked.

"Put her right by the front window," the old man said.

They walked past the door and plopped the cage down on a stand.

"No!" Zeno squawked. Bars and glass separated Zeno from the great wide world that he had never fully appreciated before now.

"Zeno want!" he squawked even more loudly.

"That's right. Keep talking." The old man sat on a stool behind a counter.

"Zeno want! Bad human. Bad bad bad. Zeno booful briyant. Zeno not pet." Zeno screeched.

The phone rang. The man answered it, "Vincent's

Feathered Friends. Vincent speaking. Why, yes, as a matter of fact, we do have a talking parrot. You can probably hear her. Hey Polly. Say something."

Vincent held the phone in Zeno's direction.

Zeno shut his mouth. He had no intention of doing anything the men wanted. He even refused to eat any of the small brown balls that Slim dumped into a dish in the cage. Zeno had no idea what kind of food the balls were. They hadn't grown on a tree or a plant. They probably were ground-up crackers that had been glued back together again.

"Pfft," he muttered. He absolutely was not going to eat them. He sat there stubbornly for a long time, refusing to pick up the brown balls. But he was trapped in a cage with nothing to do. Nothing except pick up the brown balls and swallow them. Even the ones that fell to the bottom of his cage near the piles of poop.

Had anybody seen him do that? He hoped not. He was very glad the Monk parrots weren't around to mock him. The other birds in the store—the chirpy parakeets, fancy cockatoos with extravagant topknots, darling love birds, cute canaries—were all too busy squabbling with their cellmates to care about the lone parrot by the front window.

Bunny would have cared. Bunny would have been sympathetic. Of course since Bunny was a pigeon, he might not have minded being in a cage. Unless maybe it would have bothered him even more? After all, Bunny was accustomed to flying great distances. No matter, Bunny wasn't there. Zeno was all alone.

His only refuge was to preen his feathers. They were in commotion, just like his mind. He stroked each filigree to put it back in the proper place. He bent his neck to tug at the feathers on his chest again and again—and again. Tiny tufts of gray drifted down. And so the feathers of which he was so proud littered the floor of his cage along with the poop and bits of inedible food.

A bell jangled as a woman came in the store.

"I see you have an African grey. Does it talk like that famous parrot?"

"Of course it talks. Talks all the time, right, Slim?" Vincent said.

"Sure does. It's a real smart bird," Slim said.

The woman came closer to Zeno. "It pooped in its water dish. That doesn't seem very smart to me."

Zeno glared at the woman with one yellow eye. Was it smart to keep a bird like Zeno in a cage so small that he couldn't even turn around? Was it smart to feed him round brown balls that gave him the runs?

"Well? Why isn't it talking?" the woman said.

"Why isn't it talking?" Vincent said to Slim.

"Hey Polly! How's it goin'?" Slim said to Zeno.

Zeno glared at Slim with his other yellow eye and turned his back on them all.

The bell jangled when the woman left.

"What's the matter with that dumb bird?" Vincent yelled at Slim.

"How should I know?"

"You better find out. Or maybe you're too dumb."

"I'm not dumb. The bird's dumb. That's who's dumb."

Outside the window, pigeons soared up in the sky. Zeno couldn't bear to watch them. Even those silly sparrows could fly wherever they wanted, whenever they wanted, and eat whatever they could find. But not Zeno.

He bent his head to his chest again. "Tch tch tch," he muttered. Why wouldn't the feathers stay in place? He ripped out the feather that stuck out. Then the one next to it wouldn't lie smooth. Again and again he tore at his feathers. Again and again. Nothing could soothe them or the commotion in his mind. Now it hurt when his sharp beak tore at the tender skin. A pierce of pain temporarily cut through the fog in his mind. Sadly that wasn't enough to keep him from doing it again. And again. And again.

Zeno was in grave danger. If he didn't fly, if he didn't talk, if no one said his name, then he would forget he was beautiful and brilliant. After a few more days of suffering like this, he wouldn't be a parrot anymore. He wouldn't even be a bird at all.

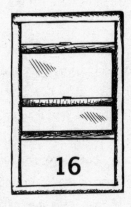

16

"The seeds Dickon and Mary had planted grew as if fairies had tended them."

Mrs. Logan read from *The Secret Garden*. A few days ago, she had found the book under the bed. After assuring Alya that there would be no dying after that first terrifying scene, Mrs. Logan had begun to read it to her.

Alya didn't mind. There was something soothing about her mom's voice—except when she tried to imitate the characters' Yorkshire accents. Something soothing about the story, too, even though it was set a long time ago. Maybe because it was set a long time ago, when fairies might very well have tended flowers instead of decorating hair accessories and teaching math in computer games.

Outside her own window, the same spring that so enchanted the children in the book was transforming the world. Yes, even in Brooklyn, trees were budding, flowers were blooming, and robins were trilling love songs to their mates.

Sometimes Alya wished that she could be wheeled into a secret garden like Colin. Fresh air and good wholesome food could cure whatever ailed him. Alya had cancer.

Meanwhile, Mrs. Logan kept reading.

"'Of course there must be lots of Magic in the world,' he said wisely one day, 'but people don't know what it is like or how to make it. Perhaps the beginning is just to say nice things are going to happen until you make them happen.'"

Alya sighed. A deep, bone-rattling sigh.

"What is it?" Mrs. Logan said, looking past the book to her own daughter lying on the hospital bed.

"Do you think there is such a thing as magic?" Alya said.

"Well, in this book." Mrs. Logan hugged it close to her for a moment. "Actually there's a great deal of magic in many books. That's why we love them."

"But in our world. Here. Now. Is there?"

Mrs. Logan tried to meet her daughter's gaze. She knew these questions were important. That made them almost impossible to answer. Each day she had to find the line between too much truth and not enough. Then she had to balance on that line. Or choose which side to fall.

The old Alya wouldn't have wondered these things. The old Alya hadn't had so much time or so much reason to ponder.

"Is there magic?" Alya sat up and stared at her mom. Her need to know was so intense that Mrs. Logan had to lower her gaze to look at the words on the page again.

Mrs. Logan found no answers there. Colin, the boy who had just recently started to walk, rambled on about Magic making the sun rise. When it didn't. The sun, to be accurate, didn't even rise. Everybody knew that.

She slowly closed the book. "The book was written a long time ago. When people hadn't learned as much as we know now. The term 'magic' was often used to explain the things that people didn't understand. However, we *can* explain them. Or scientists can."

A bird appeared at the window. It wasn't the parrot. It was the blue jay.

"I guess you could say that nowadays, in the twenty-first century, we don't need magic. We have medicine." Mrs. Logan patted Alya's legs. "It's a good thing, too. I know you hate the treatments, honey, but they really have helped you."

Alya nodded. Her doctors knew so much more than the ones who had misdiagnosed Colin.

"I'll read some more later. It's time for your power drink." Mrs. Logan stood up and carried the book to the dresser.

"Mom? Could you leave the book?"

Mrs. Logan smiled. "Of course." She put the book on the table, stroked her daughter's head for the 9,615th time and left the room.

When Alya reached for the book, the blue jay cocked its head at her and squawked, as if it wanted to tell her something. Maybe it wanted to tell her about Zeno. Unfortunately, she didn't understand "ack ack." She wasn't even sure this was the bird she had sent in search of Zeno.

She had sent Parker, too. And Parker hadn't even looked yet.

She opened the book, grateful to enter its world again. She knew she was too old to believe in magic. She wished she still could.

17

Parker stood in front of his house. He stuck his hands in his pockets like he always did when he didn't know what else to do. It had been two days since he promised Alya he would look for that parrot Zeno. Parker couldn't put it off any longer. He tried to keep all his promises—even ones he made to people who weren't sick. Only he had no idea where or even how he was supposed to look. A bunch of pigeons fluttered down and strutted along the sidewalk. They were gray, but Alya wouldn't want them.

Parker sighed. If he walked around the block, could he go back to Alya and say that he had looked? How about if he walked around it twice? Wouldn't that be enough searching? He kicked a little rock down the sidewalk. Of course that wouldn't. How could he expect her to try if he didn't?

Then he remembered one Halloween, a bunch of his friends went looking for ghosts in Green-Wood Cemetery. They hadn't found anything spooky—just a lot of wild parrots. Maybe Zeno was hanging out there.

Parker hitched up his jeans and started walking. He hadn't gone ten steps before his brain was blasting how lame his idea was. Did he know where to find the cemetery? Would the parrot be with those other parrots? Could the African grey really help his sister? No, no, and no. But finding the parrot was the only thing Alya had asked him to do for her. So he was going to do it no matter what.

After he crossed the avenue, he had another depressing thought. Even if there were a miracle, and he found the parrot, then what? Was he supposed to say, "Hey, Zeno, dude, follow me. My sister wants to see you." The whole thing was beyond dumb. Hopeless. The only thing worse would be if he ran into anybody he knew.

Then he saw the store. Actually he had passed it before he realized what it was. The neighborhood had lots of shops tucked into the ground floor of the brownstone buildings. Most of the shops sold designer shoes or baby clothes. This one had a pair of love birds cooing in the front window. The sign said: VINCENT'S FEATHERED FRIENDS.

Parker peered through the window. He thought he saw a gray parrot way in the back. It was too much to hope that it was the one Alya wanted. Maybe she wouldn't know the difference. Didn't all gray parrots kind of look alike? He opened the door and went in.

The bell jangled.

An old man sitting behind the front counter frowned, as if to say, what do you want?

Parker stood up straight and looked the man in the eye, as if Parker's pocket were full of credit cards and none of them were maxed out.

Before the old man could say anything, a huge woman pushed past Parker. She wore a multicolored jacket. Little plastic parrots dangled from her ears.

"I need a new bird," she said loudly. "Something green. But not just any green. It has to match my color scheme."

"I'll be right with you, ma'am." The old man got up from his chair and called, "Slim! Get out here. We got customers."

The old man guided the woman over to a cage full of small green parrots. "Here we have some wonderful green birds."

She took out a piece of cloth and tried to hold it close to their feathers. She shook her head. "These birds are all very blue-green. What I need is green-blue."

Slim came out of the back room, still chewing a sandwich, and stood between Parker and the shelves. Parker knew Slim was supposed to keep Parker from stealing stuff. Parker hated how nobody trusted him, just because he was a teenage boy. Like he would want those cheap plastic toys? He would have walked out, except he had to look at the African grey.

The parrot was a mess. Its head drooped. It had a huge red sore spot on its chest. Its eyes were shut. It didn't even look at Parker when he came closer to its cage. This pathetic bird would only make Alya feel worse.

"What are you hanging around here for? We don't have anything you want," Slim said.

Parker sighed. The guy was right. This place was grim. Then Parker thought maybe the parrot was all sad and messed up because it was stuck in that tiny cage. Maybe it wouldn't have been like that when it was free.

He looked at the parrot. Could it possibly be the one Alya wanted? Could it help her try? It didn't seem likely. Still, he had to be sure, so he whispered to it. "You're not Zeno, are you?"

Zeno opened his right eye.

"Are you Zeno?" Parker said.

"Pffft," Zeno muttered and shut his eye again.

"I didn't think you were." Parker sighed.

Slim came over and got in his face. "What are you doing with that parrot?"

"Nothing. I was looking for an African grey. But that's not Zeno," Parker said.

"No. It's not Zeno." Slim said the name in a mocking way.

Parker headed for the door. He had to get out of there. The place was creeping him out. He was already thinking what he would tell Alya. How he couldn't find the parrot because the parrot had joined the circus. Or teamed up with some pirates? That was ridiculous. Maybe he was helping a scientist? Yeah, that was good. Alya would be happy about that.

The bell jangled as Parker opened the door.

The sound roused something inside Zeno's brain. He blinked. He opened his mouth. Was he going to speak? Could he find the words? What were words? He couldn't remember. His world had shrunk to the size of his cage. What had that human asked him? What did the question mean? Are you Zeno? What was Zeno? No, who was Zeno? Was he Zeno? Well, was he? No, sadly, not anymore.

"Zeno," he muttered, mourning the loss of the most beautiful, brilliant bird in all of Brooklyn. It was a tragedy that Zeno had been brought to this fate. This story could have been written by one of the Greek poets. This lesson taught by one of the Greek philosophers. This tale was so momentous that Zeno couldn't suffer in silence like the stoics did. He opened his beak and wailed, "Zeeenooo!"

Parker couldn't believe it. He ran back to the cage. "Zeno? Did you say 'Zeno'?"

"Zeno Zeno Zeno!" Zeno squawked. The boy had heard him. There was hope after all. Even if Zeno wasn't completely himself now, he knew he could be again—as soon as he broke free from this prison. He beat his wings against the bars of his cage. "Zeno wants!"

All this activity got everybody's attention.

"Did that bird talk?" the woman said.

"Sure it talks. It talks great." Vincent brought the woman nearer to Zeno's cage, pushing Parker aside.

"Zeno Zeno Zeno!" Zeno squawked. He pulled himself up along the bars to try to see what had happened to the one who knew his name. Those other humans had gotten in the way.

"What's it saying?" the woman said.

"What's it saying, Slim?" Vincent said.

Slim adjusted his cap. "Um. *Sí no.* That's Spanish. For yes and no."

"It speaks Spanish?" the woman said.

"No!" Zeno squawked.

"You see?" Slim said.

"Doesn't it say anything clever? My friend Sylvia's parrot says 'Kiss me, sweetheart,'" the woman said.

"Zeno wants!" Zeno squawked.

"You see? It says plenty other really smart things, too," Vincent said.

Parker squeezed around the far side of the cage. He couldn't believe he had found the bird, but he had. He had done it. He had saved his sister. He stuck his finger between the bars. Zeno came closer to him. "Do you remember my sister? Do you remember Alya? You came to her window?

You pulled out the screen. It's still in the pine tree. Do you remember?"

"Stop bothering the bird," Vincent said.

"I'm not bothering it. It's Zeno," Parker said.

"Zeno Zeno Zeno!" Zeno squawked.

"I wish it would say something else," the woman said.

"Oh it will. It knows lots of words," Vincent said.

"Like what?" the woman said.

"My sister needs you to come. Will you?" Parker said.

Yes, Zeno did remember the girl—and the muffins. After all, they were the last ones he had seen. "Banana nut!" he squawked.

"That's cute. Of course I prefer chocolate cake. Does the bird say that?" the woman said.

"Sure, it'll say whatever you want, right, Slim?" Vincent said.

Zeno grabbed one bar of his cage and rattled it.

"How much does he cost?" Parker said.

"A bird like this? A talking bird that speaks two and probably more languages? Why, in any other store, this bird would be fifteen hundred dollars," Vincent said.

"Fifteen hundred?" Parker's jaw dropped.

"Maybe even more," Vincent said.

"My parents can't pay that much. The medical expenses are so high. She has to have more treatments. They can't pay it," Parker said.

"A thousand seems more like it," the woman said.

"They can't pay it," Parker said more loudly.

Vincent jerked his head at Slim who took a step closer to Parker.

"So if they can't, what you hanging around for?" Slim said.

"Because she needs the bird. Alya needs Zeno. She's sick. She lies in bed. She's given up. Don't you understand? She's not going to try," Parker said.

"Try! Try! Banana nut!" Zeno squawked.

"You hear that? That's why she needs him to come. Couldn't you bring him to see her? Just for a minute? It wouldn't take long. We don't live far," Parker said.

"Just for a minute?" Slim said. He had a sister. He would do just about anything for her.

"Are you crazy? What are we running here? This is a business. You want that bird to get sick from the girl?" Vincent said.

"She has leukemia!" Parker shouted the word he never said. He felt it explode in the shop. He felt the cheap plastic toys rattle on the shelves. He felt the birds succumb to a moment of silence. Then he waited, trembling, for the people who had the power to do something.

These people did not.

Vincent smiled at the woman and shrugged as if to say, *kids?*

The woman smiled back as if to say, *kids.*

Then she peered at Zeno. "Are you sure it says chocolate cake?"

"Oh, yes." Vincent smiled at the woman.

"You better throw in a year's supply of parrot pellets. And a cage."

Together they walked over to the counter where the deals were done. The woman took out her wallet and handed Vincent a golden card.

"Try," Zeno muttered.

The word hurt Parker as much as if he had been hit. He staggered toward the front of the store and got right in the woman's face. "She has cancer in her blood. Don't you understand what that means? Don't you care?"

She took a step back and made a clucking sound that she may have intended to be sympathetic. "I'm sorry. I'd love to help you, but I've got such a long drive to New Jersey. If I don't leave right now, I'll be stuck in traffic for hours on the Verrazano Bridge."

"What kind of person are you?" Parker shouted.

Vincent motioned to Slim, who grabbed Parker's shoulder. Parker jerked away from Slim and bumped into a display of little plastic birds. The stand trembled slightly, but it didn't fall, until Parker swung his fist and it all came crashing to the ground.

18

The bell jangled when the boy ran out of the shop. Zeno flapped his wings and screeched, "Zeno wants!" Where was that human going? He was the only one who knew Zeno's name. Why had he left Zeno with his tormenters? "What were you thinking?" Zeno squawked and shrieked and whistled.

Slim picked up the shelf and kicked the plastic toys out of the way.

"I could have been killed," the woman gasped.

"I should have that kid arrested," Vincent said.

Slim whispered to his boss. "Don't call the cops. Remember how I found that bird? What if somebody reported him missing?"

Vincent glanced back at Zeno, then he smiled at the

woman. "I mean, I would. But nobody was hurt. And you've still got your genius talking bird."

"You're right. I really do need to get going. Bring Polly out to my car. I'm parked right out front," the woman said.

The bell jangled again. Zeno was glad to see the woman go. He felt sorry for Polly, who was going to her car, whoever Polly was.

"Poor Polly," Zeno squawked.

Vincent and Slim came toward his cage. Was he going to be rewarded for talking? Of course! Now that they knew he was Zeno, they had to treat him with the respect he deserved.

"Kathekon!" he squawked. He was very proud of himself for remembering the Greek word that meant that everything should have its proper place in nature. "Kathekon!" he squawked again with delight as the men picked up his cage and carried him toward the door. Was it true? Yes, yes, yes, he was getting closer to the door. Then he remembered how they fooled him before when they put his cage in the window. "Kathekon!" he told them sternly.

Miracle of miracles, they heard him. Once more the bell jangled its sweet, sweet song. The men carried his cage out of the store, away from the smell and the desperate cries of the other caged birds, and into the sunshine.

"Zeno Zeno Zeno!" He was going to be free. He hardly knew what sensations to enjoy first. The trees, the sky, the clouds, a pigeon flying past—was that Bunny? He had to fly after him to see. Wait, why was he still in this cage? He tugged impatiently at the bars. "Zeno want!"

"Put it right on the backseat. Cover it up good. I don't want parrot poop all over my car."

It was that woman. Her red claws opened the car door. Slim and Vincent slid the cage onto the backseat.

"Zeno free! Zeno Kathekon!" Zeno squawked.

"See? I told you he'd say chocolate cake," Vincent said.

"Hmm." The woman wasn't so sure.

"He just needs a little more practice," Vincent said.

Slim zipped a cover over the cage.

Zeno was in the dark again. He smelled the woman's peculiar odor as she got in the car. He wasn't supposed to be going with her. He was supposed to go to the girl with the banana-nut muffin. She knew his name. This woman didn't know anything. The door slammed shut. The engine started. The car moved.

"Here we go, Polly," the woman said. "Say it again. Say chocolate cake."

Zeno wouldn't have spoken to her even if he weren't clinging to the bars with his beak.

"Chaw-co-late cake. Makes me hungry just thinking about it. Oh, there's a bakery. Do I have time to stop? Better not."

The car bumped along. Each time it swerved around a corner, he tried to remember right turn, left turn, left turn, and straight straight straight. He had to remember how to find his way back. More important, he had to remember that he was Zeno, the beautiful, brilliant Zeno. Now he understood better than most the perils of losing oneself. For he had fallen into the dark pit of ignorance. He had succumbed to self-destructive despair. But like a true hero, he had fought his way back—well, almost all the way back. There was the small obstacle of the cage, and the car, and the woman with red claws. However, he was confident that he could defeat those enemies. He was Zeno.

The car sped up and then screeched to a stop.

"I knew it." The woman honked her horn. The sound echoed from other cars. "I knew there would be traffic on the bridge. Didn't I tell that kid? He had the nerve to say I didn't care. Of course I care. I just can't get caught up in other people's problems. Besides, what could a bird possibly do?"

"Pfft," Zeno muttered. He knew what a bird could do—well, if that bird were a parrot.

The car sped up again.

"Finally we're moving," the woman said.

In the dark, Zeno narrowed his eyes and kept to himself. He repeated all the words he knew. All the things the human Zeno had said. He told himself again and again the story of the Monk parrot's Great Escape. How they burst forth from their crate with claws and beaks and a great big sound. If they had done it, then so could he.

He climbed down from the side of the cage and rested

on the bottom. The moment would eventually come. When it did, he would be ready. The woman was no match for him, even though her fingers were tipped with long, red claws. Zeno had never seen such wicked things on a human before.

"Come on, you dumb bird. Say chocolate cake."

After a sharp turn, Zeno felt his head go one direction and his stomach go another. Now he also had to concentrate on not throwing up. The car slowed down. It turned right, then left, then left, left, left. Each time, Zeno got separated from his stomach. Finally, after what seemed like forever, the car stopped. The woman got out, leaving Zeno's cage on the backseat.

Zeno shook himself all over. He lifted his left foot and extended his claws. As soon as the woman opened the cage to take him out, he would attack. He listened for other sounds. He heard birds chirping. They weren't pigeons or parrots or sparrows. Zeno squawked, "Where's Zeno?"

"Streeyet, streeyet," the birds chirped. That meant people-woods, which was what they called a suburb.

Zeno had no idea what they were talking about. He had never been in a suburb before.

A door banged. He heard the humans coming.

"How could you spend that much on a bird?" a man said.

"Sylvia spent twice as much and hers doesn't talk half so good as mine," the woman said.

"I don't care what Sylvia spent," the man said.

"Just help me get it in the house," the woman said.

The backdoor to the car opened. Big hands grabbed the cage. This was convenient. Zeno's beak happened to be near a finger. He crunched down hard.

"Yowch!" the man yelled. "It bit me!"

Unfortunately the man didn't drop the cage. Zeno was bounced up and down as the man carried him inside. Now he would be sick for sure. But no! Zeno would be brave and persevere. "Brawk!" he cried.

The cage was put on a table. The cover was pulled back. Zeno blinked at the bright light. He was in a room with lots of green-blue chairs. It was nothing like Dr. Agard's house, which had been full of books and papers and other nice things to gnaw.

"Brawwwwwwwwwk!" Zeno clung to the side of the cage and beat his wings with all his might. He spread out his scarlet tail feathers.

The woman screamed and pointed at Zeno.

"Brawk!" Zeno cried in triumph. Once again his tail had intimidated his enemies.

"What's wrong now?" the man said.

"Look at that tail! I can't have *red* in this room. It'll ruin everything!"

"Are you going to take it back to Brooklyn?" the man sounded optimistic.

Zeno was hopeful, too. He recognized the word Brooklyn.

"Don't be ridiculous. Sylvia hasn't heard it say 'chocolate cake' yet." The woman paced back and forth until something like an idea came to her. She waved her red claw triumphantly in the air. "No, I know what to do."

"What?" the man said.

She pointed at Zeno. "I'll get its tail cut off!"

19

It had been hours since Parker had left. Hours and hours since he ran down the stairs and said, "Later," when their mom asked where he was going. Alya knew. He was finally going to find Zeno. Oh, yes, Parker would keep his promise, even when grown-ups wouldn't—or couldn't.

She waited all afternoon for him to bang through the front door and run up the stairs to tell her that he had found Zeno and Zeno was on his way. She waited because, as you know, there wasn't much else she could do but wait.

Only Parker didn't come.

That didn't bother her—much. At least, not for the first hour or two. She knew it wouldn't be easy to find a bird that could fly around all over the place. Zeno didn't exactly have a cell phone they could call. It had been a kind of miracle that he had appeared at her window before.

Yes, a miracle. Could she be so lucky to have another one?

Footsteps clomped up the stairs. Her mom always tiptoed. Parker never cared how much noise he made. It had to be his feet bringing the news of what he had—or hadn't—found.

"Hi there, honey." Her dad peeked his head around the corner.

"Where's Parker?" Alya said.

"Nice to see you, too." Mr. Logan tried to make a joke.

"Hi, Dad. But where *is* Parker? He's been gone so long." Alya tried not to whine. She hated whiners.

"I don't know where he is. He just called to say he might be late for dinner. He has to go get something."

"He did? That's what he said? Exactly?" Alya sat straight up.

"I guess so. I didn't expect the third degree. I would have written it down. Would have turned on the tape recorder. Does it matter?"

Alya shook her head. The real question was, what was that 'something'? Alya shut her eyes to concentrate on hoping. Hoping required so much energy, she had to lean back against the pillow for support.

"Are you tired?" Mr. Logan fumbled with the button. The bed didn't go down; it went up. "Oops. Sorry, sweetheart. I just can't get the hang of this. Wait. Is this the right button?"

Before she could answer, footsteps thundered up the stairs and Parker came into the room. He wore a jacket. His arms were folded in a strange way across his chest. "Whoa, Alya. Way to sit up straight," he said.

Before Alya could ask anything, Mr. Logan pointed his finger at Parker and said, "*You* should try sitting up straight sometime."

Parker stared at his dad, then he turned away, like he couldn't trust himself to speak.

"Good posture is important. You walk in a room like you're proud. Not slouching. You walk in like you respect yourself, and people will respect you."

"Like they respect you. Like you've got a real job where they pay you tons of money," Parker said.

"I make enough," Mr. Logan said.

"No you don't. Not nearly enough," Parker said.

Father and son glared at each other for an entire minute until Alya made a small noise, not much bigger than a mouse. Then they both looked at her and were ashamed.

"You wanted to lie down, didn't you?" Mr. Logan fumbled with the controls again.

Parker snatched the box from his dad and fixed the bed to a more comfortable angle. Then he slouched defiantly against the windowsill.

Mr. Logan sighed. There was nothing he could do for either of his children. "I guess I'll go downstairs and see what your mother is up to."

As soon as he left the room, Alya said, "Well? Did you find Zeno?"

Parker shifted his arms a little and looked at the ceiling. "Kind of."

"You did? Oh, my gosh. You really did?" Alya sat up extra straight again, without the help of the bed. "Where was he? In the park? Is he coming to the window? He likes muffins, you know. I think you should go get him one. I hope they have the right kind. Sometimes on Saturdays the bakery runs out of my favorite. It's his favorite, too. Isn't that a coincidence? I'll give you the money if Mom won't."

"You don't have to," Parker said.

"I want to. I want to give Zeno a muffin because before, when he was here, I didn't. So now I have to. It's like I owe him a muffin. Maybe you should get two? I don't know how much he eats. He's a pretty big bird, isn't he?"

Parker nodded his head slowly, but he didn't say anything.

Then Alya got quiet. She lay back against the mattress. She felt as if the bed were sinking. She was the one who was going down and down and down. "He isn't coming."

Parker shook his head.

"He didn't want to?" Alya twisted the sheet into a rope.

"Oh, he wanted to. I mean, I know he would have wanted to."

"Then why isn't he?"

Parker frowned. He hated lying. He thought that it was

cowardly and morally wrong. Only how could he tell his sister that he had just stood there and watched Zeno get sold to a horrible woman?

"I didn't exactly talk to him. He was way up in a tree with a bunch of other parrots. So I don't think he heard me."

"You didn't shout?" Alya said.

"I did. But parrots make such a racket. Especially when there's a bunch of them. It's worse than the school cafeteria. Brak brak brak brak brak."

"You could go back. You *have* to go back."

"Sure. If you want. Only I had this idea. I mean, parrots are noisy and messy and they bite. You know Mom wouldn't allow a parrot in here. Not a real live one."

Alya stared at Parker. How could he not be on her side anymore? When did he start thinking like a grown-up?

"So since you can't have a real one, I remembered how my friend Thomas had this really cool thing."

"What." Alya's voice was flat. Like a landslide had crushed every last bit of life.

"He didn't want to let me have it. He really didn't. Until I told him that it would cheer you up."

"I don't need to be cheered up, okay?"

"Okay. Okay." Parker reached inside his jacket and fiddled with something. Then he said loudly, "Hi, Alya."

A mechanical voice said in exactly the same way, "Hi, Alya."

With great flourish, Parker pulled out a stuffed parrot. It was garish green and blue. It had puffy yellow feet and googly eyes.

"No!" Alya said.

"No!" the mechanical voice said.

"See? It talks," Parker said.

"It talks," the mechanical voice said.

Alya rolled over and pulled the pillow over her head.

Parker flipped a switch to turn off the bird. "We thought it was really funny. Of course we were, like, eight-year-old boys. And it does repeat anything, you know? Like Thomas made it burp and fart. Which is a lot harder than you think because whatever you want it to repeat has to be really loud."

"I told you why I needed him." The pillow muffled Alya's cries.

Parker squeezed the bird like he was going to rip its head off. "I know you did. I know."

20

A suitcase was on the floor in Alya's room. When Kiki and Liza came to visit, Mrs. Logan had stopped packing. Alya wished she hadn't left the suitcase open, like a diary. Underwear was embarrassing even when it was brand new.

"When are you going to the hospital?" Kiki said.

"Tuesday." The day after tomorrow. It couldn't be avoided even if it was next week or next month. Zeno wasn't coming. Alya knew that for certain even if Parker wouldn't say why.

"How long do you have to stay?" Liza said.

Alya shrugged. She honestly didn't know. She had learned not to ask these kinds of questions. She never liked the answers.

"I'm sure you'll be home soon," Kiki said.

"Oh, yes," Liza said.

"Maybe even by Friday," Kiki said.

Alya smiled politely. She didn't want to tell Kiki that she had no idea what she was talking about.

"Oh, Kiki. That reminds me. Friday is the deadline to apply for Summer Arts. Did you decide yet?" Liza said.

"What's Summer Arts?" Alya said.

"It's this amazing new camp where you get to put on plays and make scenery and costumes and learn sword fighting and everything," Liza said.

"Aren't you going to Frost Valley again?" Alya said.

"Kiki always wants to do the same thing. Don't you think it would be more fun to do something different this summer?" Liza said to Alya.

Alya had always been in favor of new adventures—but not the ones she was about to have. She dipped her head lower to hide her face under the bill of her cap. She couldn't see Kiki bug her eyes at Liza for saying such a stupid thing. And she couldn't see Liza's mouth crinkle because she was so sorry.

"I like your cap," Liza said. "It's cute. Is that a parrot?"

"It's the wrong kind." Alya took off the cap and stared at the colorful macaw. Her mom had been so excited to find it tucked away in the suitcase closet. The remnant of a summer vacation. "Do you want it?"

"Oh, no. It's your cap," Liza said.

"I have lots. Take it." Alya held it out.

Liza shook her head almost like a shudder. "I don't really like caps."

Alya didn't, either. The difference was that Liza didn't have to like them. They were a fact of life for Alya. She turned the cap around and around in her hands. She felt her friends staring just beyond her left shoulder, waiting for her to put the cap back on.

Kiki and Liza knew something was wrong. They didn't know what. They would never know about the trying or the not trying, and Zeno and Parker, and why this cap with the wrong parrot was the worst possible thing in the world, and yet Alya had to put it on.

So she did. And Kiki and Liza breathed again.

"You can have my soccer ball," Alya said.

"What?" Kiki said.

"Take it. It's in the closet," Alya said.

Now Kiki shook her head at Alya. "Why are you trying to give away your stuff?"

"Because it's dumb to have everything just sitting around here when you could be using it. So take it. Liza can have my boots."

"Your boots?" Liza said.

"You know you always liked them."

Liza did like Alya's boots. They were such a dark purple that they almost seemed black. Each side had a little elastic, so they were easy to slip on even though they were real leather riding boots.

"Take them. They're in the closet, too."

"Stop it, Alya. Liza isn't going to take your boots." Kiki spoke firmly because she could see that Liza was tempted.

"I can't wear them. It's dumb to wear boots in bed." Alya tried to laugh.

"You aren't going to be in bed forever," Kiki said.

"How do you know? Are you a doctor?" Alya said.

Silence settled over the room. The gray spread out from the unpainted corner like an ominous cloud.

"Did you read *The Secret Garden* yet?" Kiki said.

"Yes," Alya said.

"Isn't it the best book ever? Don't you just love Dickon?" Kiki said.

"Are you crushing on him?" Liza said.

"You have to love a boy who talks to animals," Kiki said.

"It isn't real. That magic stuff doesn't work like that in real life," Alya said.

"Of course it isn't real. It's a book." Kiki picked it up from Alya's dresser and held it close to her. "I'm sorry you didn't like it."

"I liked it okay." Alya couldn't look at either friend. She picked at a little thread at the edge of the blanket. She pulled it even though there was a chance that she would unravel the whole thing.

Kiki and Liza exchanged a look that meant, should we leave?

"Well," Liza said.

Alya wished they would go. At the same time, she was afraid they would leave her and never come back.

"I know. I know. You have to go. You have homework. You have to take out the trash and clean up your rooms before you go to soccer practice and walk with all your friends to the corner store to get a snack," Alya said.

Kiki didn't say anything.

"The corner store is closed. For renovations," Liza blurted.

"Again? Why do they keep trying to fix it up? I mean, it's a corner store." Alya tried to joke. She wanted so badly to smile so they could leave thinking she was the good old happy Alya. "Like what are they going to do? Put in marble floors?"

"Maybe mahogany shelves," Kiki said.

"All the lights will be crystal chandeliers," Liza said.

"No, no. I know. Each package of Ring Dings will be displayed on a pedestal," Alya said.

Kiki and Liza laughed. Then it really was time for them to go. Hugging over the bed rail wasn't easy, but they did it.

"We'll come and see you in the hospital," Kiki said.

"We'll bring you flowers," Liza said.

Alya felt her smile freeze into a Halloween clown mask. Please don't bring flowers, she thought. She didn't want to watch them die.

21

From the living-room window, Parker watched Kiki and Liza skip down the stairs and over to the sidewalk. At the gate, they turned to look back at the house. Then Liza's cell phone rang. She looked at it and grabbed Kiki's arm. They ran down the sidewalk. Were they in trouble? Were they excited? Did it matter? Alya wasn't with them. Alya couldn't be with them, and it was Parker's fault. He should have just stolen Zeno. So what if they sent him to prison? He could handle it. He'd rather be in prison than look at Alya and know that he had let her down. He had failed. He should be punished, not her. It wasn't fair that she had to stay at the hospital just because of a bunch of steps.

He flopped onto the sofa. Suddenly he jumped up again and looked out the window at the six steps leading up to the house. He counted them carefully, then he ran up to Alya's bedroom.

"Alya," he cried.

"What?" she said.

He panted a little, from excitement and running so fast. "You don't have to go to the hospital on Tuesday."

"Are you going to cure me again?" Alya said.

"No, you have to go for the treatments, but you don't have to stay there."

"You know I can't make it up all those steps." Alya could barely look at him. Why was he torturing her with this kind of talk?

"You don't have to go up *all* of them. Just the six to the front door. Then you can loll around on the sofa watching TV until I get home from school and carry you the rest of the way." Parker grinned. He was very proud of his idea.

"Just six?"

"Yep." He showed Alya six fingers.

Even though he needed to add the thumb from his other hand, it still didn't seem like very many. "Six," she said again.

"You can do six."

That was easy for him to say. When he climbed six steps, he only did two because he always jumped over the second, the third, and the fifth.

"You really think I could?" Alya stuck her fingers in the unraveled part of the blanket.

"Yes. I know I didn't get Zeno to come. But maybe that's okay. Maybe he already taught you what you need to know."

"You think?" Alya looked at Parker.

"Come on. I'll take you downstairs so you can practice."

Before she could say yes or think no, Parker lowered the railing and scooped her up. He carried her all the way down to the front hall.

Alya stood next to the bottom step and looked up the staircase. She counted the six steps. She reminded herself that six wasn't even as many minutes in an hour or hours in a day or days in a week. Six was hardly anything.

She took a deep breath and put her hand on the bannister. Then she let go of it and grabbed Parker's arm again.

"I better do it later. When I'm not so tired," she said.

Would there ever be a time when she wasn't?

Parker returned Alya's hand to the bannister. "I think you should climb the stairs *now*."

Now was not nearly such a nice word as tomorrow. *Now* could only be right away, but tomorrow could slip and slide into nearly *never*. And *never* was a terrifying word.

"Okay. I'll do it," she whispered.

Mrs. Logan hurried out of the kitchen. Her hands were wet; she hadn't taken the time to grab a dish towel. Bubbles dripped onto the floor. "Do what?"

"Alya's going to practice climbing six steps. If she can

make it up the stoop, she won't have to stay at the hospital," Parker said.

"Sweetheart, are you sure you can?" Mrs. Logan asked Alya. "What if you fall?"

"She won't fall," Parker said.

"But what if she does? What if she gets hurt? Then they'd have to wait to start the treatments. And we don't want that, do we? Honey, I know you'd rather not stay at the hospital, but it's only for a little while. Dr. Jones said it really was a good idea to have you right there in case anything bad happened."

"The bad thing is she can't hardly walk. That's what's bad!" Parker yelled.

Mrs. Logan bit her lip. She couldn't argue with that.

Parker patted Alya's shoulder and said, "Go on. You can do it."

"Wait!" Mrs. Logan rushed into the living room and returned with orange pillows from the sofa. She put them on one side of the stairs.

Mr. Logan came out of his office and looked down at them from the landing. "What's going on?"

"Alya's going to climb the stairs," Parker said.

"She is?" Mr. Logan sounded shocked.

"She's going to try," Mrs. Logan said. "But Parker will be right there to catch her if she falls."

Alya meant to try. She really did. She lifted her right foot. She put it on the first step. Then she couldn't remember what to do next. Push with her leg? Pull with her arm? As she turned toward Parker, she wobbled a little.

Mrs. Logan gasped. Mr. Logan ran down all fourteen steps so fast that he nearly crashed into his children. Parker moved Alya out of the way. Then he and Alya tumbled onto the orange pillows.

"Are you all right?" Mrs. Logan said.

Parker picked up his sister and carried her to the sofa.

"Alya, sweetie, are you all right?"

Mrs. Logan had to keep asking because Alya didn't answer. She could barely hear her mother. She had crawled into a dark cave.

"You were right. You *were* tired. You can try again tomorrow morning before I go to school," Parker said.

Alya sadly shook her head. There would be no more trying. What was the point? She had failed. She couldn't climb even one step. She would never ever climb six. Her mom was right. It was safer to stay at the hospital while she had the treatments—and maybe even for the rest of her life.

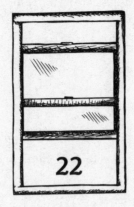

22

*C*ut? What was *cut*?

What was that terrible woman with the long red claws going to do to him? Zeno didn't know. He was in the dark. Really and truly. He had squawked so much that the woman had put a cover over his cage. He kept squawking no matter how many times she told him to go to sleep. Sleep? How could he sleep? He was in terrible danger. *Cut?* What was *cut*?

He rattled the bars of his cage and tried to prepare for a Great Escape. What had the ancestors of the Monk parrots done? They burst from their crate with loud screeches and claws. Unfortunately, when Zeno tried to hurl himself at the side of his cage, he bumped most painfully into the bars.

"Yowch," he cried. He had forgotten an important part of the story. The Monk parrots burst forth only *after* a man had opened the crate.

So Zeno crouched on the floor of his cage and waited for the woman to come.

He waited.

And waited.

And waited.

Wouldn't she have to feed him? Shouldn't she bring him water?

"BRAWWWK!" he screeched.

"Shut up or I'll trim your tongue, too! You know that bird hasn't said one actual word since I got it. It certainly hasn't said 'chocolate cake,'" the woman said.

Trim? What was *trim*?

He was in a commotion again. He didn't know what to do. He bent his head to preen the feathers on his chest. Of course, the feathers weren't there anymore—just his tender skin. He wanted to smooth them. He couldn't smooth them. He had to do something. He couldn't do anything. He was trapped. Just as he had been in the store. His situation had only gone from bad to worse.

"Zeeeenooooo!" he moaned. He was losing himself again. He had to escape. He couldn't escape unless she opened the door. He waited. He couldn't wait. He seized the bar of the cage with his beak. He gnawed the metal. He would never break the bar, but at least it was better than gnawing his own skin.

❧ ⟡ ❧

Day came. He saw the light change.

He heard the woman approach. She would feed him. She had to feed him. And then she would open the door. He would be ready. He crouched on the floor of the cage and prepared to spring up at her face.

The woman lifted the cloth. "Oh, that red tail looks even worse today. Thank goodness the groomer can come tomorrow. He can clip your wings, too."

She had food in her hand. She was going to open the door. Zeno braced himself.

She threw a handful of brown pellets through the bars. They rained down on Zeno. "There."

"BRAWWK!" Zeno screeched. This wasn't the proper way to feed a parrot.

"Shut up!" She dropped the cloth over the cage. "I better keep you covered. I can't stand to see your tail anyway."

Tap, tap, tap. Zeno heard the sound of her shoes leaving.

He shook himself. Brown pellets fell from his feathers. He was too upset to eat. *Groomer*? What was *groomer*? *Tomorrow*? When was *tomorrow*? He had to get out of the cage, the cage, the hated cage. He had spent so many hours in it.

He knew every bar, every cross piece. He hurled himself at the door again. This time, he felt a sharp pain. A small wire poked his body. He attacked this little piece of wire with his beak. He tugged at it. He twisted it. He would get rid of it. He would rip it off the hinge and . . .

Then he stopped.

He tapped the little wire with his beak. Then he felt along the side of the door. Each side of the rectangle had three more wires. Three and three and three and three were all that attached the door to the cage. He returned to the first one, the one that poked him. He twisted it once more. It fell to the bottom of his cage with a very satisfying little clink.

Now that side only had two. A moment later, there was one. And then none.

Zeno trembled with excitement. He bobbed his head up and down, yes yes yes. He would escape. And what's more, his escape would be greater than the Monks' Great Escape because he had to do it all by himself. He didn't have the help of a flock. And he didn't have the help of a human. However, that didn't matter because he was, "Zeno Zeno Zeno. Booful briyant Zeno!" he screeched.

The cover lifted. The woman's face peered at him. "What did you say? Did you talk?"

Zeno blinked. He shifted slightly away from the door.

"Come on. Talk. Say 'chocolate cake.' Chaw-co-late cake."

She poked him with one long, red claw. Would she notice the door wasn't shut as tight as it had been? Would she notice the little metal bits among the poop and the pellets on the floor of his cage? Would she notice anything at all?

Zeno flashed his red tail.

"Stop that." The woman shuddered and dropped the cover back over the cage.

Tap, tap, tap. The sound of her shoes faded as she left the room.

"I just had a brilliant idea. I bet those gray feathers could be dyed. Then I could get the exact color of green-blue that I need. I'm going to call that groomer right now."

Green-blue? Like a Monk? Zeno was horrified. He got right back to work on another side of the door. The first wire came right off, but the middle wire was twisted so tightly that he chipped part of his beak. It was a small price to pay for freedom. Zeno flung that wire out through the bars. It clinked as it fell to the floor.

Zeno froze. Would the woman come? Would she discover his plan? He listened. He heard nothing except strange sounds that came from the next room. Bursts of music, glass breaking, people shouting, people laughing, engines roaring. Zeno didn't know what the sounds were. However, he didn't let them distract him from his goal. The third side was free. The door to his cage would soon be on the floor with the pellets and the poop. The cloth cover, why, that was nothing, he was actually looking forward to shredding it. Soon he would be outside his cage—and trapped in the room of the house.

Crushed by this realization, Zeno let his head fall to his chest.

All that work. For what? He may have been the most beautiful, brilliant bird in all of Brooklyn. His beak may have been incredibly strong and agile. But he would never be able to open a human door. Never ever ever.

He poked at the tender part of his skin. That pain didn't hurt nearly as much as the realization that he had failed. His tail would be cut. His wings would be clipped. His feathers would be dyed green-blue. He would certainly no longer be Zeno.

He actually lay down on the bottom of the cage, in the poop and the pellets and the little bits of wire. In the shadowy gloom he watched the cage door swing back and forth on its last remaining twists of wire. It mocked his previous hopes and dreams. So you thought you could be free. Didn't you know that there is always another cage? And another and another and another. A cage, a room, a house, a city. Wasn't life itself a kind of cage?

What would Zeno the human have to say about that?

Nothing. Maybe that was why Zeno the human decided to be stoic instead of fighting against fate. Maybe he knew he couldn't win.

Zeno the bird lay on the floor of his cage all night, and shut his eyes to the darkness.

The next morning, he could hear birds singing to greet the new day. Of course they were joyful. Why shouldn't they be? They would soon be flying to find food. They weren't waiting for a groomer to come inside the house and clip, cut, trim . . .

"Brawk!" Zeno squawked.

He sat up. He shook his feathers. He flapped his wings. He bobbed his head. Yes yes yes, he was. He was waiting for a groomer to come inside.

"Brawk!" He blinked. He kept his eyes shut. He had to remember the room. He couldn't quite. The woman came and went from two directions. Which was which? He gnawed a tiny hole in the cloth. That was better. Yes. Now he could see. One way was where she kept her food. The other way wasn't. Yes yes yes, now he was ready, so he waited for the groomer.

He waited the forever that you always have to wait when you are waiting for something important.

Finally the doorbell rang.

Zeno blinked.

"Coming!" The woman's silly sandals tip-tapped past Zeno's cage. *Tap, tap, tap,* across the hall toward the front door.

"I'm so glad you could come this morning."

She was talking too much. She always talked too much.

He couldn't hear. He needed to hear. Everything depended on it.

"I can't bear to wait another minute to get rid of that hideous red tail."

The lock clicked. The hinges squeaked. A bit of breeze came in the room as the woman pulled open the front door.

"Come in, come in," she said.

The wire door clattered to the ground. The cloth floated up.

A gray streak zoomed past the woman and the groomer—and up into the beautiful blue sky.

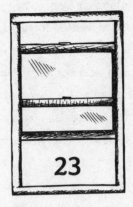

23

Zeno was free. Yes, free! He flew up, he flew down, he flew east, he flew west. He landed on a branch. He snapped off twigs. He hopped on the ground. He drank from a pond. He ate beetles. He did everything he wanted to. He even did some things he had never wanted to before—such as talk with a flock of sparrows taking a bath in the dirt.

"Preep," they chirped, which meant, *preep*.

"Zeno free! You free!" Zeno squawked.

"Preep preep," they chirped. *Whatever.*

Their lack of enthusiasm wasn't surprising. No one had ever put *them* in a cage.

"Free good good good," Zeno squawked as he flew away again. He was much too excited to try to explain anything to sparrows.

He flew north, he flew south, he flew right, and then hurried back the other way again when he thought he saw the woman's house. He wanted to get as far away as possible from those red claws. He flew out of the woods, past more houses, across a very wide road with lots of rushing cars. He flew and flew until he reached a type of land he had never seen before—a big flat area of nothing but brown dirt. All that empty space made him nervous. Where was he? He had no idea, except that he was free. Yes, free!

He looked for a place to perch. Being free was exhausting—and just a little bit frightening.

Along the edge of the road there were tall poles connected by wires. Zeno came to rest on top of one of those poles. He panted a little. He would have liked a nice drink from the shiny bowl in Dr. Agard's kitchen. Or from a puddle. Or from the pond by the Parrot Man. However, he would never have to drink from that dish in his cage that sometimes had poop in it. Because he was free!

A car sped along the road. Zeno was glad it didn't stop. He didn't want to see any humans ever again. And yet it felt strange to be so alone. It seemed like there was nothing in the whole world except brown dirt.

"Pffft," he muttered.

He wasn't lonely. That queasy feeling in his stomach was hunger. The tightness in his throat was thirst. How could Zeno be lonely? He was Zeno, wasn't he? Of course he was. He had himself. After all, what was a friend anyway but "another I"? That was what the human Zeno had said. And the human Zeno had been right about almost everything.

"Kathekon!" Zeno squawked. All his words came back to him—especially the Greek one that meant things should be in their proper place. He had been restored to his—the top of a pole where he could look down upon everything.

He preened his feathers, taking great care to stay away from the wound on his chest. He had learned his lesson. He concentrated on his tail. Oh, how close he had come to losing it. He stroked it gently. It was a beautiful tail. Dr. Agard had often said, "Zeno, you have such a beautiful tail."

"Zeno booful tail," Zeno squawked. Somehow that didn't sound quite as wonderful as when Dr. Agard had said it. It was always better when someone else called you by name.

The boy who had come into the store had called him Zeno. If he hadn't, Zeno might never have remembered who he was. "Zeno Zeno Zeno!" Zeno squawked.

The boy had shouted at the humans and knocked over the shelf. He had been very upset. Of course he had. Zeno had been upset, too. Zeno was in a cage. Zeno wasn't free. Zeno would have knocked over all the shelves and bitten the humans. The boy should have done that. He had teeth, even if he didn't have much of a beak.

The boy had said something else. Zeno cocked his head. Then he remembered. The boy had a sister. The sister knew Zeno. The sister was sick. That was why she wanted Zeno.

"Girl want Zeno," Zeno squawked.

Then he blinked. It was something more than wanting. He wanted a lot of things. Mostly food. His time in the cage had taught him what it meant to need.

"Girl need," Zeno muttered. He turned his head upside down. Then he nodded, yes yes yes. The girl needed Zeno. "Girl need Zeno! Zeno free. Free free free."

Yes, he was. He could go to the girl now. He could do whatever he wanted.

"Zeno fly Brooklyn!"

He flapped his wings vigorously as if getting ready to fly straight to the girl. And if he got to eat a muffin, well, so much the better.

"Banana nut!"

There was just one problem. He couldn't fly to Brooklyn. He didn't know where it was.

"Pfft," he muttered.

He looked right. He looked left. He looked down. He looked up. He didn't see anything remotely like Brooklyn.

Far far above him, higher in the sky than he had ever dared to go, another creature made lazy circles in the sky.

The creature circled lower and came to rest two poles away from Zeno. It was a hawk. The hawk stared at Zeno. Zeno stared at the hawk. Neither bird blinked for a very long time.

The hawk had brown feathers. Its beak wasn't as grand as Zeno's. Nor did it have those distinctive white circles that made Zeno's eyes look wise. The hawk did have a red tail. Of course it wasn't nearly as vivid as Zeno's scarlet tail. Still, it was red.

The hawk didn't speak.

Neither did Zeno. And yet there were many things he wanted to ask this bird who had flown so high and who sat on its pole with such imperious posture. Where did you come from? How can you fly like that? Where did you get your red tail? Might you perhaps be "another I"?

"Zeno!" Zeno thought he should identify himself.

The hawk didn't speak.

Maybe the hawk couldn't speak? Not all birds chattered away like the Monks. Zeno wouldn't have minded a silent friend. (To be honest, Zeno believed that when the human Zeno said "two ears, one mouth," he meant that others should be quiet and listen to Zeno talk.) And yet there was something unsettling about the way the hawk looked Zeno up and down. As if the hawk were measuring Zeno's size and strength—and whether Zeno would be good to eat.

"Brawwk!" Zeno showed his strong beak as he flapped his wings and flashed his scarlet tail, which meant, *Don't even think about it.*

So the hawk didn't. He shifted his head to search in a new direction.

A van came along the road. It stopped between Zeno and the hawk. A man got out and slammed the door. Zeno got ready to fly away from this human, but the man never looked up at Zeno. He stared at his watch for several minutes. Then he yanked open the back door of the van.

A cloud of birds flew out from the back and up into the air. The man waved his arms excitedly and shouted, "Go, go, go! Beat that Louis Lazar!"

The man watched the pigeons for a moment before he got in the van and drove back the way he came.

The flock swooped and swirled together in one motion. It was hard to see what kind of birds they were. Then Zeno realized they were pigeons. He remembered that the ones he met in Brooklyn had flown a hundred miles. Could these be the same pigeons? Zeno couldn't tell.

"Brooklyn?" Zeno squawked.

The pigeons paid no attention to him. The spiral widened as they figured out which direction to fly.

How did they do this? Of all the ways they could go, how did they choose? They didn't follow a road. They couldn't read highway signs. They carried no maps. They had no access to global positioning systems. What guided them again and again back to the place from whence they had come? Humans didn't really know, even though they had used pigeons to carry messages since the days of the human Zeno in Ancient Greece. Did the pigeons steer by the sun? Did they detect the earth's magnetic force field? Or did some other sense whisper to them—this is the way to go home.

Yes, home.

The pigeons settled on a course. A dark gray one was in the lead. The flock was in tight formation, all except for one. A white pigeon with brown wings was having trouble keeping up. It had a bit of the flu and probably shouldn't have come on this race.

Was it Bunny?

Zeno cocked his head. Before he could fly closer for a better look, the white pigeon was seized by the long yellow talons of the hawk.

24

The white pigeon shrieked with pain as the hawk's talons dug into its flesh. The rest of the pigeons circled back toward the white pigeon.

Zeno was glad that they were going to its rescue. He had just recently survived a dangerous adventure. He couldn't possibly take on another. Besides, he wasn't one-hundred-percent sure that that was Bunny. Didn't all pigeons look alike? Even white ones with brown wings?

"Brroo, brroo," said the white pigeon, which meant, *Fly away to safety, my friends.*

The other pigeons didn't obey. They chased after the hawk and tried to slap it with their wings. The hawk flew steadily on, clutching its prize. The pigeons' feathers didn't even tickle. Again and again, they hit the hawk with their wings. What else could they do? They had no weapons to fight a hawk. Their beaks were for pecking. Their red feet were for hopping.

The hawk carried the white pigeon toward Zeno's spot on top of the pole. The white pigeon fluttered one brown wing. It was still alive—for the moment. The harder it tried to shake itself free, the tighter the hawk squeezed.

Zeno had never witnessed a killing. He certainly didn't want to see one now.

Then the hawk carried its prey almost directly above Zeno's head.

"Brrrooo brrrooo," the pigeons said. *Leave Bunny alone.*

So it *was* Bunny. Yes. Zeno could see that now. He could also see the terror in Bunny's eyes.

Come on, pigeons, fight for your friend, Zeno thought.

"Brrrooo, brrrrooo," the pigeons said. *Please don't hurt Bunny.*

"Pffft," Zeno scoffed. Was that the scariest sound those pigeons could make? Couldn't they even attempt a decent screech? How in the world did they ever expect to win any battles in this world without sharp weapons or, at the very least, a big mouth?

"Brawwwk!" Zeno squawked.

All eyes turned toward him.

"BRAWWWWWWK!" Zeno cried again, even louder than before. His battle cry lifted him up off the pole and into the swirl of feathers. As he flew, he stretched his gray talons out to their most dangerous extent.

"Ker-chee!" the hawk cried out in surprise as Zeno grabbed its left shoulder and stabbed at the hawk's neck with his beak.

"Ker-cheeeeee!" squealed the hawk. It released Bunny and flew off across the field to find another meal—one without such a powerful friend.

Bunny fluttered to the ground. The rest of his flock joined him. They cooed and rubbed one anothers' necks. Then they looked up at Zeno, who was once again perched on top of the pole.

"Brrooo brrrrooo," they said to one another, which meant, *Can you believe our friend Bunny was just saved by a parrot?*

"Zeno," Zeno squawked. He thought they'd want to know his name, even if they could never pronounce it properly. He assumed that the pigeons would *brroo* on and on about the battle. How the pigeons had failed to save their friend. How brave Zeno had attacked the hawk (even though Zeno was fatigued from his earlier triumph in which he had escaped from a human with dangerous red claws). How brave Zeno had used his brains and his beak to save poor Bunny.

"Brroo," Bunny said. *Thanks.*

"Tens?" Zeno squawked. What was Bunny talking about? "Tans? Tins?"

Believe it or not, Zeno didn't know the word "thanks." His ignorance could only partially be excused because Bunny's voice was hoarse from the attack—and all the pigeons had extremely thick Brooklyn accents.

Bunny corrected Zeno, "Brroo, brroo, brroo." *Thanks, thanks, thanks.*

"Brrroo," the other pigeons said. *Save your breath.* They said it in the nicest way. Bunny did need to save his breath for the long journey ahead.

"Brrooo?" the dark gray pigeon said. *Ready?*

The rest of the flock rose up into their spiral.

"What?" Zeno squawked.

"Brroo," Bunny said. *Home.*

Bunny flapped his wings and joined the flock.

"Home?" Zeno muttered. That word was familiar. Then he remembered. Long ago, on the rooftop in Brooklyn, Bunny had tried to teach Zeno about home. Zeno hadn't understood the concept back then. Well, sometimes it's hard to know what you have until it is taken from you. Zeno had to be kidnapped, nearly lose his tail, and escape to a vast empty field before he finally understood what Bunny had told him. Home meant friends like Bunny. And, of course, food.

"Wait!" Zeno squawked.

The pigeons didn't. The spiral flattened into a triangle as they flew toward Brooklyn. Nothing else mattered now that they knew they were going home.

"Home!" Zeno squawked as he hurried to catch up to them.

"Home! Home! Home!" he said it several more times. He was always proud to have learned a new word, particularly one as important as this.

25

"Tail. Booful tail. Bad woman want cut. Cut cut cut!"

The African grey parrot and the white pigeon with brown wings flew side by side above the road.

"Zeno briyant. Zeno Great Escape. Zeno bite door. Zeno free," Zeno squawked loudly. There were more cars driving beneath them now and he wanted Bunny to hear what he was saying. "Free good! Free Kathekon!"

Bunny bobbled his head in agreement. Even though he didn't know the Greek word, he did know that birds were supposed to be free and not in the clutches of hawks.

Zeno thought the same thing and squawked, "You free! Free good! Free fly home. Zeno fly. Bunny fly."

Bunny was indeed flying, and that was why he didn't speak. He wanted to save his breath. Having flown this distance before, he knew the journey would be long and difficult without many good places to rest.

"Zeno caught. Bad man. Zeno cage."

Zeno, on the other hand, was not taking the pigeons' advice. He had much too much to say. Think of all the adventures he had had. He was so happy to have someone to tell them to. Since Bunny was a pigeon, Zeno kept his sentences simple. He didn't want to impress Bunny with his 128 words. He wanted to be understood.

"Sick babies. Feed them, Zeno cry. Men bad. What were you thinking? Zeno hurt. Zeno not Zeno. Boy come. Boy say girl need Zeno. Zeno Zeno Zeno!"

Could you blame Zeno for chattering on and on? He had discovered the joy of sharing his thoughts and feelings. And what an unmitigated delight it was—or would have been if his companion had been strong enough to speak to him in return.

Bunny communicated as best he could. He looked encouragingly at Zeno as they flew along. Zeno beamed back at him, never taking his right eye off Bunny. As a result, Zeno didn't know what Bunny felt with each weary flap of his wings—the distance between them and the rest of the flock grew longer and longer. And longer.

Bunny tried so hard to close that gap. Of all the pigeons in that flock, he had the most heart. In other words, he never quit. Never ever. He wasn't quitting then, either. He worried about the parrot, who, as Zeno himself often said, was *not* a pigeon and consequently would not know how to find his way home.

The two birds turned away from the setting sun. As they flew toward a huge highway, Zeno noticed that Bunny's wings beat much more slowly than they had when the journey began. To tell the truth, Zeno was extremely tired, too. He had to admit that pigeons were stronger fliers than he was.

"Pfft," he muttered. Of course, he hadn't spent his days racing a hundred miles. He had discussed Greek philosophy with Dr. Agard.

"Follow where reason leads," Zeno squawked.

Bunny nodded in agreement. Reason was leading them home.

They flew on and on until they came to a wide river. The wind swirled above the water in unexpected ways. Each time Zeno tried to glide on top of an air current, it switched course on him, and blew him back the way he had come. He flew lower to avoid the wind. To his surprise, he found Bunny flying even lower still, on a path that seemed to head dangerously near the water.

"Try!" Zeno squawked.

Bunny did try. Somehow he struggled on. But as soon as they had crossed to the other side, Bunny dropped down to land on a most uninspiring patch of dirt.

Zeno landed next to him and stood for a while with one foot in the air. He really didn't want to put his foot down in the mud.

Bunny couldn't go any farther to a nicer place. He shook his head at Zeno and jerked his beak in the direction of the other pigeons. "Brroo," Bunny whispered. *Fly on ahead.* Then he bumped Zeno with his wing to make his meaning even clearer. Zeno should hurry and catch up to the flock—or he might not make it home.

"Not fly home?" Zeno blinked.

Bunny nodded.

"Pfft," Zeno muttered. He didn't want to fly with the others. They were only pigeons, after all. But Bunny, well, Bunny was Bunny.

"Brroo." Bunny bumped Zeno again. Bunny told Zeno to leave Bunny to rest, he would find his way home eventually, in a day or so. Zeno had to follow the flock now, just in case Bunny would be unable to show him the way.

Actually Bunny couldn't say all that with just a "brroo." He didn't need to. The birds understood each other perfectly. In fact, with all of the words at our disposal, we couldn't have illuminated the situation much better than when Bunny said, "Go," and Zeno said, "No," and plopped his entire body down next to Bunny.

And so, as the flock continued on to Brooklyn, the African grey parrot and the white pigeon with brown wings sat on the dirt.

To be honest, Zeno wasn't being completely selfless as he stayed with his friend. (Well, he was about sitting on the dirt. He would have much preferred to perch practically anywhere—even on the rim of that trash can.) Zeno didn't understand the problem. He had complete confidence in his own ability to continue the journey.

Once again, Bunny urged Zeno to join the others. This time, with a blink of his eye, for he had lost his ability to make a sound.

"Zeno need Bunny. Bunny need Zeno." Zeno gently rubbed his beak along the back of Bunny's neck. He finally understood what the human Zeno had meant when he said a friend was "another I." Zeno knew that he cherished his friend as much as he cherished himself.

"Friend," Zeno squawked.

Bunny nodded his head in agreement.

Although the sun had disappeared beyond the western bank of the river, the sky didn't lose its light for a long time. A rosy orange glow emanated from where the sun had set. Yet, you could be forgiven for thinking that some of that glow came from the place on the uninspiring patch of dirt where two brave friends faced the ultimate challenge—together.

As Bunny sank into the most profound kind of silence, Zeno spread his wings and squawked. "Brawwwwk!"

Unfortunately death couldn't be scared away. It took Bunny, no matter how fiercely Zeno flapped his wings and flashed his scarlet tail.

26

Mrs. Logan stroked Alya's forehead for the 9636th time. Alya shut her eyes to pretend her mom's hand shushed all the bad thoughts away, just as she had done when Alya was little and monsters lived under her bed. Alya didn't believe in those monsters anymore. She had other ones to worry about.

"I know you're anxious about going to the hospital tomorrow, but it won't be so bad. You can bring all kinds of things to decorate your room to make it seem like home."

Oh sure, it could *seem* like home. And Alya could *seem* like Alya—if she wore her cap and remembered to smile.

"You can put up pictures on the walls. I know, we can hang the big banner that was signed by everybody in your class." Mrs. Logan picked up a roll of brown paper.

Alya sighed.

Mrs. Logan put it back in the closet. "What about the poster of the coral reef? Or the map of the world?" Alya just stared at her mom. "I don't know what you want. You have to tell me."

"I want to stay here," Alya said.

Mrs. Logan looked at the bookshelf. "Is there a book you'd like to bring? You gave *The Secret Garden* back to Kiki. Which of these haven't you read yet? Of course there will be lots of kids to talk to. You won't be as lonely as you are up here all day. I'm sure you'll make tons of new friends. You were always so good at making friends."

Mrs. Logan didn't notice that she had said "were," as though that happened in the distant historical past. Alya noticed. Of course the old Alya made friends. The old Alya was always doing something exciting. But the new Alya? Well, the new Alya was going to be living at the hospital.

"You think about it while I finish up." Mrs. Logan took pajamas out of the middle dresser drawer. She folded the sleeves to show the picture of the cute kitten on the front. Then she refolded them because they hadn't come out even.

The room was silent. You couldn't even hear a bird chirp. Mrs. Logan worked very hard on the packing. Alya worked very hard on not crying.

"It's only for a few weeks," Mrs. Logan said again.

That was how long Alya had to have the treatments. Nobody ever said anything about what Alya would be like when the treatments were done.

"It got dark so fast. I wonder if a storm's coming. Do you want me to turn on the light or are you going to sleep?"

Alya's eyes were shut, so Mrs. Logan let the room remain in shadows. However, Alya had no intention of sleeping on her last night at home.

Zeno moved away from the body of the bird lying on the dirt. He perched on the rim of a nearby garbage can.

A storm was coming. Zeno felt a charge in the air. Off in the distance, where the sun had disappeared, monstrous clouds roiled in the sky.

A smaller bird, or a wiser one, might have been frightened enough to take the nearest shelter in a rickety building between the patch of dirt and a big field. Zeno didn't know what to do. He felt like all his feathers were ruffled, even the ones he didn't have anymore. He had been flying home with Bunny. Now that Bunny had gone, had home gone, too?

"Home?" Zeno muttered. "Friend food. Food friend. Food food food."

The trash can upon which he perched contained several delicacies—a packet of french fries with just a dribble of ketchup, a box of popcorn, and half a hot dog bun. The bun was of the same texture and color as a you-know-what. Zeno wasn't even tempted. He had learned that hunger came in different forms. Now all he wanted was to go home. He flapped his wings and soared up in the air.

"Brroo brroo," he imitated the pigeons perfectly. Then he squawked, "Zeno home."

The African grey parrot flew all by himself in a spiral, just as he had seen the pigeons do. Once, twice, three times around. However, his ancestors didn't whisper to him.

"Home?" he squawked.

His friend was no longer there to guide him. But he remembered the direction that he and Bunny had been flying. Zeno was quite certain that that was the way to go. So he flew straight east, away from the land known as Staten Island—and out over the Atlantic Ocean.

The winds whistled past the pine tree in the backyard. Luckily Alya couldn't see the dark clouds massing like enemy troops at the edge of the night sky. Listening to the wind was frightening enough. It sounded like the world was coming to an end. Then she realized that her world really and truly would come to an end, once she lived at the hospital.

What could she do? Nothing. She had tried, hadn't she? She just couldn't climb the six steps. Nobody had really believed she could. Not even Parker. Her parents had been so worried that she would fall, so of course she fell. Now she felt like she was still falling, deeper and deeper into a hole.

27

Zeno worked very hard to fly in a straight line. Could he see a bedroom window? Could he see a girl lying in her bed, waiting for him to come? No, but he was confident that he would soon. And, as you know, Zeno never thought he was ever wrong. So he flew east, directly toward a group of little islands called the Azores—over two thousand miles away.

The storm caught up to him. The wind splashed water in Zeno's face. "Brawk," he spluttered. He blinked to clear his eyes. He looked down.

What had happened to the land? It was completely gone. No road, no field, no patch of dirt, nothing but a tumult of dark waves. He had never seen so much water in all his life. Where had it come from? He sank a little as he flew lower than he should. A white wave reached up and grabbed

Zeno's wings. He panicked and flapped frantically to push himself higher.

What if he needed to rest? Where could he perch? He had to head back toward shore. But which way was the land?

He flew to his right. That was surely wrong. He flew to his left. Was that right? He was flying in circles. Each time he slowed a little to think, the wind tossed him as if he were nothing but its plaything. Oh, it was terrible. Now he wished he could see the other pigeons. But he was all alone. One bird caught between the sea and a stormy sky.

"Zeno!" Zeno squawked.

Would he ever get back to land? Or would he fly endlessly through the dark?

The bad thoughts crept out of the gray corner. There were more than usual. And they all had plenty to say. The sick kids wouldn't like her. The nurses would have schedules. The lab technicians would have long sharp needles. She would miss her family. How could Parker cure her if he couldn't hear her crying in the next room?

"Please go away," she whispered to the thoughts.

She tried lying still, hoping they wouldn't notice her. She was, as you might remember, very good at lying still now.

The thoughts kept coming.

She pulled the covers over her head to hide. The blankets just trapped those thoughts with her in the hospital bed. Nothing good was ever going to happen to her again.

If only Zeno would come in the window like he had done before. Only he wasn't going to. Or was he?

Her nose itched, so she rubbed it. Hard.

Then she made a discovery. It was as important as finding a new planet or a new species of singing whales. She discovered she could still believe in good things.

She pushed back the covers. It was hot under there and stuffy and boring besides. She kicked her feet free of the blankets. She sat up and crawled to the end of the bed to push the covers onto the floor. Then she slid through the gap between the railing and the foot of the bed.

Luckily her mom wasn't there to send Alya back to bed right this instant before she caught a cold. Mrs. Logan would have said, "What on earth are you trying to do?"

Could Alya have answered? Probably not in actual words.

She stretched out her hands to steady herself and took several stumbling steps away from the bed. She didn't fall. In fact, she felt some strength return as she walked across the room.

Maybe believing wouldn't help you get things like never having homework on holidays or your very own horse that you could ride whenever you wanted. But believing was absolutely essential when you had a battle to fight.

She leaned against the sill to rest for a moment. Then she grabbed the handles on the sash and pulled up with all her might. It was quite a struggle. Her arms quivered. Her heart pounded. Her face was hot and red. She wanted to give up, but she didn't. She raised up the sash. Drops of rain splattered against her face. She felt invigorated by the wind. She didn't care that she got a little wet. She knew she had to open the window so that Zeno could come back to her.

And now she believed that he would.

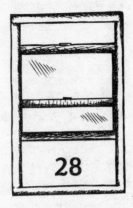

28

Of course Zeno didn't know what Alya had done. How could he? He was many miles away. He wasn't even thinking about Alya. He was in a panic. Land? Where was land? Fly? How could he fly? His wings were so heavy he could hardly lift them. He was beyond exhaustion. He had already flown fifty miles. What was worse, he had no idea where to go. The dark night was made darker by the storm. He was lost over the ocean. His only companions were the fierce wind and the driving rain.

"Zeno want," he muttered.

Yes, his favorite words. Except that now, all he wanted was to rest.

"Zeno want," he murmured.

Once more the waves tried to pull him into their embrace. The ocean water seemed warmer than the cold rain.

Why should he keep fighting the storm? Why should he try when it seemed certain he would fail?

And then, for some reason, he thought of the girl. She hadn't tried.

Or had she?

Maybe that was why she sent her brother to find Zeno. Maybe she wanted to fight. And if she could, then so could he.

"Zeno want," he said again.

The wind lifted him up above the waves. Before it let him fall, he beat his wings with renewed purpose.

He formed a picture in his mind of the girl who needed him. He thought she could be his friend—even if she didn't have the banana-nut muffin anymore. He concentrated on making his way to her, much as pigeons do when they have to find their way home.

"Home," Zeno muttered.

He realized that he had been going the wrong way. Somehow, as if he could see the girl standing in the open window, he knew he should turn left. So he did.

"Home," he said, a little more loudly.

Maybe you think he should save his breath. Didn't he need to hoard every drop of his energy? Each time he opened his mouth, more of the storm came inside him. And yet, strangely enough, just feeling that word vibrate inside his body seemed to give him new strength. "Home!" Zeno squawked. "Home, Zeno, home!"

Then he saw lights. Yes, far, far ahead of him there were bright dots in the sky, sometimes hidden by the clouds. They seemed so distant that they couldn't have been made by men. They must have been stars strung across the sky. Only he knew they weren't. They couldn't be. They were his only hope.

On and on he flew. The closer he got, the more lights appeared. A long curved smile of lights. Then the clouds parted and he saw that smile connected the towers of a very tall bridge.

The Verrazano-Narrows Bridge had been built high enough so that ocean liners might sail in from the Atlantic Ocean and come to rest in one of New York City's harbors.

And so Zeno the bird flew up under the bridge and came to rest on one of its girders.

Many other birds were already there, taking refuge from the storm. All the birds had fluffed out their feathers for warmth and tucked their heads under their wings to sleep. Most were seagulls, but there were also blackbirds and even a few pigeons.

Zeno clung to the edge of the beam as he shook the water off his feathers. He was so happy to have made it this far; however, a girder under a bridge wasn't home. He wondered how much farther he had to go. "Brooklyn?"

None of the birds answered him. Could you blame them? Every bird there had been battered by the wild weather.

"Help parrot Brooklyn home?" he squawked as nicely as he could considering that neither the storm nor his friend Bunny had taught him how to say please.

Still no one pointed a beak in the right direction.

"Girl want Zeno?" Zeno said.

A few of the birds blinked in recognition. So this was Zeno. The news had spread from bird to bird about the girl who foolishly wanted the parrot.

"Zeno want girl."

The birds nodded in amazement. Astonishingly enough, now the parrot wanted the girl.

The oldest gull pointed his long yellow beak in the direction that most of the cars were traveling. Zeno took a deep breath and set off again.

He flew under the bridge to stay dry for as long as he could. Then he followed the cars as they sped along the wide road. The rows of buildings all crammed together looked familiar.

"Brooklyn!" he squawked.

Yes, he was actually in Brooklyn.

The rain had stopped. The gray sky hinted at morning. When it was the color of Zeno's wing feathers, he flew over a section of Brooklyn without houses. The green field was full of small gray statues—some were humans with parrot wings.

"Brawk!"

It was Green-Wood Cemetery. He would have liked to

rest on top of the Parrot Man, but he didn't want to run into those round-headed Monk parrots. He didn't want them to mock him for flying so far to help a girl. But that was what he had done.

He flew past the Parrot Man and down a street and around a corner. And there it was. He saw the pine tree. The window screen Zeno had pulled out was still stuck in its lower branches. There was the window guard he had perched upon the last time he had seen a banana-nut muffin. There was the window. He flew toward it, planning to rap on the glass. Only the window was open, so Zeno flew in.

29

The girl looked at the parrot.

The parrot looked at the girl.

"Hello, Zeno," Alya said.

"Hello, Zeno," Zeno squawked.

Alya felt a little shy, so she put on her plaid cap. "You're bigger than I remember."

Zeno flapped his wings and showed off his scarlet tail. "Zeno booful briyant bird."

Alya smiled. "Yes, you are." Then she noticed the wound on his chest. "What happened to your feathers?"

Zeno bent over the place that would always be tender even though the skin was starting to heal. "Zeno not free. Zeno not Zeno," he muttered.

"I understand." And Alya did, for she had been to a dark place herself. She took off the cap and stroked the top of her head. The tiny black hairs were still easier to feel than to see.

Zeno blinked. He turned his head to one side and made the most soothing sound he knew. "Brrooo brrroo."

Alya smiled. "But you're free now, right?"

"Zeno free. Girl free. Free good." Zeno hopped onto the table and rapped the wood sternly with his beak. "Banana nut! Zeno want!" He was starving after his long journey. He cocked his head and fixed one yellow eye on Alya.

"Are you hungry? Of course you are. I'm sorry I don't have the muffins anymore. I can get you some other food. Or my mom can." Alya knew she would never make it to the kitchen and back upstairs again. After all, even believing had its limits. Then she remembered. "I think I have something you can eat."

She pulled herself up and shuffled around the monstrous bed. In the back of her second drawer, behind the socks and the frilly pajamas she never wore, she had hidden some candy from last year's Halloween, before there had been any desperate adventures for either Zeno or Alya.

The candy was six months old. Most of it was things like sour balls and jaw breakers that Alya hadn't wanted to eat. There was one packet of almond M&M's.

"Aha!" Alya sat down on the floor. She opened the bag and carefully sucked the chocolate off one piece. She offered the nut to Zeno.

Zeno cocked his head to one side and then the other to

examine the small brown thing. He preferred to eat food that was dry. However, anything would taste better than those cracker balls. He picked up the thing with his beak. He wrapped his tongue around it. It felt like an actual nut. He chomped on it and swallowed. "Nuts!" he squawked.

He ate the rest as fast as Alya could lick off the chocolate. After the last one, he hopped back onto the railing around the bed and spread his wings to show her his tail.

"I still can't believe you're really here," Alya said.

"Booful tail, bad red," Zeno squawked.

"What do you mean, bad red? I love your tail," Alya said.

"Cut cut cut," Zeno squawked.

"Cut?" Alya said.

Zeno bobbed his head, yes yes yes.

"You mean cut your tail? That's terrible. How could you fly without a tail?" Alya said.

"Great Escape. Zeno free," Zeno said.

"I'm so glad you did. Where were you, anyway?" Alya said.

"Fly hundred home," Zeno said.

"A hundred? You don't mean miles, do you? How could you fly so far?"

"Brrrooo brrroo." Zeno perfectly imitated Bunny again.

"A pigeon? I see them swooping past my window all the time. Could they fly that far? Unless you mean a homing pigeon?"

Zeno nodded his head, yes yes yes. A pigeon who knew about home. Then he said, "Brroo brroo," again and solemnly lay down on the table.

"Oh. Did something happen to a pigeon?" Alya said.

Zeno stood up and blinked several times. "Zeno friend."

"I'm sorry." Alya extended her finger.

Zeno looked quizzically at it. He turned his head upside down to look beneath it. No nuts. "Pfft," he muttered. And yet he knew the finger was offering him something important, so he gently rubbed the side of his beak against it.

Suddenly the bedroom door opened. Zeno flew up to a safer place.

Mrs. Logan entered carrying a tray with a glass of that pink liquid. "Here's your energy booster, sweetie. I hope you can drink it all. You'll need your strength for . . ."

She gasped. The bed was empty. Her daughter was gone. A gray bird perched on the railing and flapped its wings. Mrs. Logan dropped the tray. She thought the winged creature might be a soul ascending to heaven.

"Brawk!"

Did souls squawk?

Parker raced into the bedroom, followed by Mr. Logan.

"It's Zeno!" Parker said.

"Zeno Zeno Zeno!" Zeno squawked.

"He came, Parker! He came," Alya said.

"Hey, Zeno! I'm so glad you made it, man." Parker offered up his fist.

Zeno bumped it with his beak. "Cut cut cut! Great Escape. Home. Banana nut!" Zeno squawked.

"You mean he still wants those muffins?" Mrs. Logan said.

Zeno bobbed his head, yes yes yes, of course he wanted muffins. He always would, no matter how many escapes he made or what dangers he survived. He especially wanted to share some muffins with his new friend.

"Girl want. Zeno want. Banana nut," Zeno squawked.

"What's he saying?" Mr. Logan said.

"Could you get us some muffins please, Dad?" Alya said.

"I'll go to the bakery." Parker raced down the stairs. He knew he would be much faster than his dad. And *he* wanted to be the one to bring the blue-and-white bag for Zeno.

The whole family sat on the bedroom floor and ate. Zeno was a messy eater. Mrs. Logan didn't complain that the crumbs went everywhere. She was grateful to see Alya enjoying food again.

When the muffins were gone and Zeno had shredded the paper bag, Alya stood up to announce, "I'm ready."

"We don't have to go to the hospital quite yet," Mrs. Logan said.

"To climb the six stairs. Parker, I need my horse," Alya said.

Parker whinnied and knelt so Alya could climb on his back. As he carried her downstairs, the parents hurried after them. Zeno perched on the bannister.

Alya stood in the front hall and took a deep breath. She let go of Parker and gripped the railing. She stood for a moment. Was she remembering how she had failed? Was she worrying that she wouldn't make it?

"Maybe you can try later. You've already done much more than you . . ."

Zeno interrupted Mrs. Logan. "The wise are earnest in self-improvement."

"What's he saying?" Mr. Logan said.

"Try!" Zeno squawked.

Alya put her foot on the first stair and pulled herself up. She took another step, and then another and another until she had climbed all six. She only wobbled once, at the very end, when Parker's hug nearly knocked her down.

She sat on the sixth stair. Her heart was pounding. She was worried about how she would react to the chemotherapy. She knew it would be hard to go back into battle. She was grateful for one thing. "So after the treatment today, I can come home?"

Mrs. Logan nodded. She was crying and couldn't speak.

Zeno had to say, "Home home home."

30

The splendor of this moment ended abruptly when Mr. Logan glanced at his arm and cried out, "Oh, no, look at the time!"

"We'll all be late!" Mrs. Logan said.

Time? What was *time?* *Late?* What was *late?* Zeno wondered. The humans were quite afraid of these things. They all ran off frantically in many directions, except Alya, who couldn't run. She stayed where she was, anxiously jiggling her hands as she called to her mom.

"Where's my book and my tunes? Did you fill my water bottle? Don't forget the crackers. Not the cheesy kind. They make me feel worse."

The commotion made Zeno so nervous that he was glad to follow Parker out the front door. Parker ran up the street, but Zeno found a suitable spot on the branch of an oak tree right next to the house. After several more minutes of shouting about the dreaded time and the terrifying late, Alya came out of the door, dressed in different clothes and wearing her plaid cap.

"Hello, Zeno," Zeno squawked.

"Hello, Zeno," Alya said. "I was wondering where you went. You'll be here when I get back, won't you? You'll be here when I have to climb the six stairs?"

Zeno nodded his head, yes yes yes. He liked the tree. The branch was strong. The bark was rough. It was a good place for a parrot.

Then a car stopped in front of the house. Zeno flapped his wings and cried out in alarm. He didn't like cars. "Bra-wwwk!" Alya didn't understand the danger. She and Mrs. Logan slid into the backseat. The car drove away.

"Brawwwwwwwk!" Zeno cried again.

Alya couldn't hear him—but someone else did. Vack had been on his way to a pine tree he enjoyed. Now he glided down to perch just above Zeno's head.

"Brak brak brak," Vack said. *What were you squawking about?*

"Brawk," Zeno squawked. *You wouldn't understand.*

"Brak brak," Vack said. *Oh yeah?*

So Zeno told him the story of Alya and the muffin. And of Zeno's own Great Escape from the woman with the red claws who took him away in a car. And of his battle to save his friend Bunny from the hawk. And how Bunny's last thoughts had been about helping his friend Zeno get home.

"Brak?" Vack said, which meant, *Home?*

For that was a word the Monks knew well.

Zeno bobbed his head, yes yes yes. Home. Then he told how he very nearly hadn't survived that stormy journey across the Atlantic Ocean. But he had fought on because he knew he needed to help Alya. And he *had* helped her. And she had been so happy. Only now she had disappeared into one of those cars. And he didn't know when she would be back.

"Brak brak brak," Vack said, which meant, *Humans like to ride in cars.*

"Pfft," Zeno muttered. *I knew that.*

"Brak brak brak brak brak," Vack said. *Humans like to be in their cages. Parrots like to be free. Unless they are pets.*

"Brawwwk!" Zeno protested. He was nothing of the kind.

"Brak brak brak," Vack said. *Did the girl feed you?*

Zeno glared at Vack, as if to say, *So?*

"Brak brak," Vack said, which meant, *Then you are her pet.*

"Zeno not a pet!" Zeno squawked. To prove it for once and for all, he flew up from the oak tree, away from the six steps that Alya had yet to climb, away from the bedroom where there were still some crumbs from the banana-nut

muffins that Zeno and Alya had so thoroughly enjoyed—
away away away to find a place where he could be left alone.

Vack was wrong about a lot of things. For instance, Alya
did *not* like riding in the car after spending all day getting pumped full of strong medicines. Every single bump in
the street—even the tiniest ones—jiggled the contents of
her stomach and threatened to undo the precarious balance
between staying down and coming up.

Mrs. Logan squeezed Alya's hand and kept saying,
"We're almost home. We're almost home. We're almost
home."

Finally they were home. The car stopped. Mrs. Logan
helped Alya out of the backseat. Alya hurried as fast as she
could toward the oak tree. She looked up. She moved her
head to the right and then to the left, hoping to see something hidden by the branches.

"Hello, Zeno," Alya called.

But Zeno wasn't there.

She stood at the foot of the six stairs. Mrs. Logan stood
next to her, with her arm around Alya's shoulder.

"Hello, Zeno," Alya said.

Mrs. Logan moved her arm so that it was around Alya's
waist.

"Hello, Zeno," Alya whispered.

Mrs. Logan put down the bag containing the book, the water bottle, and the crackers, which Alya had been unable to eat, so that she could hold her daughter with both arms.

Alya chewed her lower lip.

Mrs. Logan awkwardly reached around Alya to get out her phone.

"Who are you calling? Zeno doesn't have a phone." Alya tried to make a joke.

Mrs. Logan wasn't ever very good at punching the buttons with just one hand. She especially wasn't good when she felt her daughter sinking. She tried to guide Alya to sit on the lowest step. Alya wouldn't budge.

"He doesn't have a watch, either. I didn't tell him what time to be here. I didn't think he could tell time. Except I could have said, when the sun has moved past the roof."

Alya looked up. She didn't see the sun. She saw clouds. Darker than the gray of a parrot's feathers.

"This is Parker Logan's mother. I think he's in biology class this period. I need him to come home right away. It's an emergency."

"No!" Alya said. "Don't call Parker. Parker has to stay in school. He has a big test tomorrow."

"I know he has a test tomorrow. But he can come today at least."

The clouds darkened. Or was it just the mention of that tomorrow, when there would be more strong medicine.

"Zeno will be here. I told him to wait and he nodded that he would."

Mrs. Logan slowly shut her phone. "Alya, he's a bird."

"I don't care what he is. He understands me. Why else would he fly all that way to come back?"

"He probably just wanted the . . ."

Mrs. Logan didn't say it. She pressed her lips together. Then she kissed the top of Alya's plaid cap and kept her mouth there so she wouldn't be able to say something that would be the final blow to a terrible day.

She didn't need to say it. Alya was already thinking the same thing. Zeno hadn't been her friend at all. He had only cared about the banana-nut muffin.

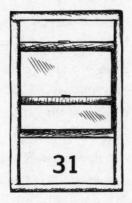

31

The rain came. It fell hard all over Brooklyn. It rattled against the roofs of the brownstones. It beat on the red umbrella Mrs. Logan had hurriedly fetched from inside the house. It flattened the hair on Parker's head as he ran down the block to where his sister sat waiting on the step. It soaked the grass in Green-Wood Cemetery. It bounced off the stone wings of the Parrot Man and up against the tender place on Zeno's chest.

Zeno felt miserable. His feathers were wet. His feet were cold. He took whatever shelter he could from his wing and waited for the storm to pass. The rain lasted all through the night and darkened the dawn. Eventually the sun did come out. He spread his wings and spent hours removing the drops of water from his feathers with his beak. By the end of the day, he was completely dry. And he still felt miserable.

He was hungry. Well, he was always hungry. So the next day he went in search of food. It took him all morning to discover that the inside of a pine cone was actually pretty good to eat. He ate his fill. And still he felt miserable.

He didn't like sleeping on the Parrot Man. So he moved to the branch of a nearby tree that provided more shelter from the winds and some nice bark for whenever he felt like having a little gnaw. And he still felt miserable.

Maybe, just maybe, the misery was inside him. But what could it be? He bent his head toward his chest. A few tiny feathers were just beginning to peek up through the skin. He knew that place would always be sore.

"Zeno not Zeno. Zeno not free," Zeno muttered.

Only this time, no one said, "I understand."

The girl who had lost her feathers, too, wasn't there.

He blinked several times. Where was she? Was she still in the car? Or had she come back?

"Girl want Zeno," he squawked. And then he thought, but didn't say, Zeno want girl.

So he flew back to the girl.

At first, he couldn't seem to find the right window. All the houses in that part of Brooklyn looked alike. How had he ever found his way to her before? Then he remembered how Bunny had taught him to concentrate on returning to food and friends—and home.

Zeno flew along the park and turned slightly toward the setting sun. Yes, there was the pine tree. The screen was still stuck in its branches. There was the window up on the third floor. Zeno flapped up to perch on the railing to look inside the room.

Something wasn't right. The big bed with the shiny railings was gone. The girl wasn't there. The room was completely empty except for a large, lumpy shape in the center, shrouded in white cloth. There was a strange, piercing smell. But Zeno was brave. He had a strong beak and a loud squawk. He could battle these unfamiliar enemies. The window was open, so he flew inside.

Parker was kneeling in the corner of the room carefully smearing thick globs of blue paint over the gray.

"Hello, Zeno," Zeno said.

Parker stood up so fast that blue splattered across the floor. "You're here! You're here! Alya will be so happy. She's been so worried about you. She thought someone had captured you and put you in a cage again."

"Zeno free. Zeno not pet," Zeno squawked.

"Of course you're not. I'm so glad to see you."

"Girl want Zeno?" Zeno squawked.

"Yes, she does. She really does. If only she could be here."

"Girl want Zeno!" Zeno rapped his beak sternly.

Parker put down the brush and wiped his hands on his jeans. "Alya got an infection. So she has to stay at the hospital to get antibiotics."

Zeno narrowed his eyes. He didn't understand those words, but he knew he didn't like them. "Home home home," he squawked.

"I know. I want her to come home, too." Parker's voice cracked. "It's hard, man. Because I really want to go in there and bust her out. You know?"

Zeno knew all about Great Escapes. "Free free free."

Parker shook his head. "She needs extra medicine to fight the infection. The only way to get it is to stay in the hospital. So she has to. Sometimes you can't push or bust stuff up. Sometimes you just have to wait. And hope. And get rid of that hospital bed. And paint this room so that if she does come home . . ." Parker wiped his face with the back of his arm. "No, *when*. When she does come home."

Parker turned to Zeno with a strange look in his eyes.

"Zeno, this time, when she does come home, you've got to be here. You've just got to. I know you're only a bird. Nobody blames you. It wasn't your fault it was raining. She probably would have gotten sick anyway. That happens with leukemia. Her white blood cells can't fight diseases. And the treatments make her even weaker. That's why you have to be here for her. She needs you."

What were these words? Zeno didn't understand them, either. *Sick?* What was *sick? Blood?* What was *blood? Blame you?* What was *blame you?* And why was that human hand reaching behind Zeno's back? What was the boy going to do?

198

"Brawwwk!" Zeno bit the hand before it could grab his body. "Zeno free! Free free free!" He screeched as he flew away.

"Wait, Zeno!" Parker ran to the window. It was too late. Zeno was gone. Parker stared at his hand for a moment, like how could *it* have been so stupid? He smacked it against the freshly painted wall.

Parker didn't tell Alya what had happened. He was too ashamed—and afraid. How could he add this news about Zeno to the strong medicine that slowly dripped into a tube and traveled to an opening near her heart?

He did his best to tempt Zeno to come back. Every morning, before he went to school, he left a muffin right outside Alya's bedroom window. Every night, when he came home, he studied the pile of crumbs. Was that the footprint of a parrot? Was that one of his small gray feathers? Was the piece of paper shredded in the shape of a Z?

Finally he had to tell Alya. He couldn't afford to wait any longer. His conscience was bothering him too much. And as you know, muffins didn't grow on trees.

He sat by her hospital bed. He described how Zeno had flown in the window looking for Alya and how Parker had scared him. "By accident. I didn't mean to. I'm so sorry. I should have known you can't hug a bird."

Alya didn't say anything for a moment. She didn't say much these days. Her illness had taken most of her strength. But somehow she was able to find the good inside the bad. Somehow she pushed away her worries to come to the realization. "Zeno came looking for me."

"That's right. He did. He wanted to know where you were. Don't worry. You'll see him again. I'll keep putting out the muffins for him."

Alya smiled. "He didn't just want the muffins. He really did want *me*."

"Yes." Parker put his arms around his sister. He was grateful that he could hug her.

Finally the treatment was done and Alya came home. Parker carried her up the stairs to her room. Mr. and Mrs. Logan followed. Parker swung open her door with a great flourish. Her bedroom had been transformed. The hospital bed was gone. In its place was one with bamboo posts. The walls were one-hundred-percent blue. He had painted the corner three times to make sure that not even one small speck of the gray remained.

"It's wonderful," Alya said.

"Parker did it all," Mrs. Logan said.

"Dad added the palm tree," Parker said.

"There was kind of a bare spot there," Mr. Logan said.

"He wanted to keep decorating. But I told him you might like to do some of it yourself," Mrs. Logan said.

"You just let me know if you want me to paint anything in that tree," Mr. Logan said.

Mrs. Logan gave him a stern look. They all knew he was about to say, like a big African grey parrot with a scarlet tail.

Alya shook her head. She got up from the bed and walked over to the window. She tugged at the sash. Parker came over and helped her raise it up.

She picked up the piece of paper littered with crumbs. She carefully folded the paper and handed it to Parker. Then she said, "I better let Zeno know I'm back." She leaned out of the window and called, "Hello, Zeno."

She called a little louder. Why should she be embarrassed about wanting to find her friend? "Hello, Zeno!"

She took a big breath and let that name sing out over the roofs of the brownstone houses, through the tops of the trees, past a swirl of pigeons who had journeyed an unbelievably long way and were almost home. "Hellooooo, Zenoooooo!"

Her words soared up into the sky that was as blue as the walls in her bedroom. Up and up and up until they were met by something gray streaking across the sky almost as fast as a jet.

It wasn't a jet, however. It was an African grey parrot, whom you already know.

Zeno flew into the bedroom and perched on the bamboo bedpost. He was very pleased to see it. Wood was much nicer than those metal bars that surrounded that other bed. He looked forward to some delightful gnawing. But at that moment, he preferred to sit on the girl's shoulder.

He took off her cap and tossed it to the floor. Her feathers hadn't grown back yet. "Pfft," he muttered.

"Hello, Zeno," she whispered. She tentatively stroked the back of his neck.

"Hello, Zeno," he said, just like he always did. Except that many things had changed—not just the color of the walls and the bed. He had traveled such a long way. And so had she.

He twisted his neck so that he could look at her face. She was his friend. She was another I. But she wasn't Zeno. She was . . . what? He bumped her nose with his beak. "Hello? Hello?"

"Alya," she said.

"La-ya," he corrected her pronunciation. "La-ya La-ya La-ya." He had learned a new word. Now he knew 129. He was extremely proud of himself. After all, La-ya wasn't just a word, it was something more important. La-ya was a name. No, wait. La-ya was his friend's name.

"Hello, La-ya." He had so much to tell her; he didn't know where to start. He had had so many adventures since he had seen her last. Then he turned his head upside down to study her. She must have had adventures, too. He wanted to hear all about her Great Escape from the car and her cage. But first he needed to know if there would have to be any more escapes.

"La-ya home?" he said.

"Yes." She nodded, yes yes yes.

Acknowledgments

I'm grateful to Dr. Irene Pepperberg, whose research and collaboration with Alex inspired me to write about an African grey parrot. To my husband, Lee, and my daughter, Sofia, for their wisdom and support. To my mom, Virginia Kelley, for listening. To Rachel Berger for her insights on an early draft. To Susan Westover and librarians everywhere who work so hard to connect kids with books. To my agent, Linda Pratt, for her enthusiastic guidance. To everyone at Feiwel and Friends. And especially to Liz Szabla, my amazing editor, who enriched this book in so many ways.

GOFISH

JANE KELLEY

© Keith Weber

What did you want to be when you grew up?
I wanted to be an actress. My childhood seemed kind of ordinary to me. Being in plays gave me a chance to live other, more-exciting lives. I studied theater in college. After I graduated, I performed with a street theater company for many years.

When did you realize you wanted to be a writer?
When I was in my early thirties, I discovered that writing was another way to be inside of a character. Plus, as a writer, I had much more control. I could choose who that character would be. I no longer had to wait to be asked to create.

What's your most embarrassing childhood memory?
When I was in the fourth grade, a group of girls always bullied me on the school bus. One day, they shot spitballs at me. That was pretty humiliating—and gross. I was tired of being picked on, so I decided to throw one of their spitballs back at them. Unfortunately, the bus driver saw me. So I was the one who got yelled at, and they just laughed.

What's your favorite childhood memory?
I loved playing in the woods behind our house and on our neighborhood beach at Lake Michigan.

As a young person, who did you look up to most?
My grandmother, Katharine Carson, who was a novelist. She died when I was six. But other family members always spoke of how wise and talented she was, so sometimes, I would imagine the sort of counsel she might give me.

What was your favorite thing about school?
Spending time with my friends! I liked being in shows and playing the flute in the school band. I was a good student, but I don't recall being as excited about learning things as I am now.

What were your hobbies as a kid? What are your hobbies now?
I spent a lot of time hiking, camping, swimming, and canoeing. I played the piano, the flute, and the guitar. Being outdoors and making music are still important parts of my life. I'm in a community chorus. Singing with other people is a wonderful feeling. The group makes me sound much better than I ever would on my own.

Did you play sports as a kid?
I wasn't on any teams because I didn't believe I was athletic. When I got older, I found that I really enjoyed tennis. It's very satisfying to hit the ball hard—and keep it in the court.

What was your first job, and what was your "worst" job?
My first job was working in a factory in our basement. My father invented things in his spare time. One product was a

portable greenhouse called the Gard 'n' Gro. Our whole family assembled them and got them ready to be shipped all over the country.

My worst job was being a waitress. I had to quit after just a few weeks—I couldn't handle being nice to people who were complaining about their food.

What book is on your nightstand now?

Several! Naomi Klein's *This Changes Everything*—a nonfiction book about the connection between climate change and capitalism. *Death by Toilet Paper*—a funny and poignant middle-grade novel written by my friend Donna Gephart. And *The Signature of All Things*—Elizabeth Gilbert's novel about a woman botanist.

What sparked your imagination for *The Desperate Adventures of Zeno and Alya*?

I read a news story about Alex, a real African gray parrot who was being studied by Dr. Irene Pepperberg. Her experiments with Alex proved that parrots actually thought and felt; they didn't just "parrot" what humans said. I became obsessed with those parrots, but I couldn't have one as a pet. My cat wouldn't have liked that. So, I decided to write about one. I'm not sure why I imagined that parrot flying into the bedroom of a sick girl. But I often start writing with two ideas that don't seem to fit together. If I keep thinking about them, eventually I discover how they connect.

Have you ever been on a desperate adventure yourself?

Fourteen years ago, I had breast cancer. The year of treatments was definitely a desperate adventure. I'm happy to say that they worked; I'm fine now. But there were dark days when I wondered if I would ever be anything but a cancer patient. Those feelings became part of Alya's character.

What was the most difficult scene to write? What was your favorite scene to write?

It was really hard to describe Zeno's days in the pet shop, when he had forgotten his name and was tearing at his own feathers. I didn't even know parrots did that until I started researching them. Just as with humans, boredom and isolation can make parrots turn against themselves.

I loved writing the scene where Bunny the pigeon helps Zeno finally understand the true meaning of the word "friend."

What kind of research did you have to do to write this novel?

My research was so much fun. I really love learning new things. I read lots about parrots, including Dr. Pepperberg's book, *Alex and Me*. I watched the videos people posted of their parrots on the Internet. I studied the pigeons from my window. (My cat helped me do that.) I hung out in the nearby cemetery to observe the flocks of monk parrots that live there. And I read about Zeno, the Greek philosopher.

What was your favorite part of writing from the perspective of a parrot? What was the most challenging part?

Flying! I really loved imagining what that felt like for all the birds.

The most challenging part was being true to the birds as birds. Some novels treat animals as humans in costumes made of feathers or fur. I wanted to dig deeper, if I could. I hoped I could expand our understanding of another species. That's what books do best—enable us to look beyond ourselves.

What makes you feel better when you're sick? What do you do for your loved ones when they are sick?
When I was little, the most comforting thing was when my mother read to me and stroked my forehead. I carried on that tradition whenever my daughter was sick. And of course, I made many cups of tea and pots of soup.

Who or what most motivated you to complete this novel?
My belief that this story would be comforting to those who struggle to hang onto their identities—and inspiring to those who need to hear a rather raucous voice shout, "TRY."

What's your favorite saying or philosophy by Zeno?
"A friend is another I." Of course, the parrot Zeno doesn't understand that at first. He thinks the quote means that all his friends should be just like him. But I believe treating others as we wish to be treated ourselves is the most important basis for civilization.

What is your favorite word?
Quest. It means a journey and a search. What could be better than that? It's also part of the word "Question." And it starts with a Q, a very valuable letter indeed.

Who is your favorite fictional character?
Charlotte in *Charlotte's Web* by E. B. White. She is wonderful and wise—and she knows how to get things done.

What was your favorite book when you were a kid? Do you have a favorite book now?
Jane Eyre by Charlotte Brontë. I found it wonderfully encouraging that a smart, plain girl (who happens to be named Jane) gets love and respect in the end! Now that I'm older, I

admire Marilynne Robinson's Gilead trilogy. Her writing is so beautiful. And her generous spirit is so comforting, especially when she tackles difficult topics.

What's the best advice you have ever received about writing?
Keep writing. Love the process. Find joy in what you can do each day.

What advice do you wish someone had given you when you were younger?
I wish someone had told me I didn't need to wait for permission to write. My thoughts were just as important as anyone else's. I just needed to keep working at the best way to express them.

What do you want readers to remember about your books?
My books are all very different, and yet I do return to certain themes. I write about the importance of nature, the power of believing, and the need to keep trying.

What do you consider to be your greatest accomplishment?
I have a remarkable daughter and a wonderful partnership with my husband. But Sofia and Lee had a lot to do with those successes. My own greatest accomplishment is giving voice to how someone else felt. I'm really grateful to the readers who have told me that I've done that.

What would your readers be most surprised to learn about you?
That, unlike Zeno and Alya, I don't really like banana nut muffins!

Would you dare to undo a spell?
To save your friend?

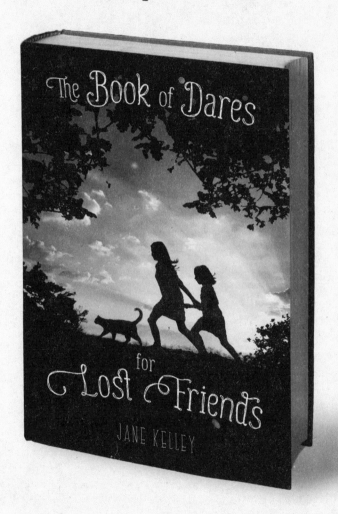

Keep reading for a sneak peek!

One

A sleek, black cat walked along the sidewalk. She held her tail high. A shopkeeper shouted at her. Three little children called, "Oooh, kitty." She didn't even look in their direction. She paused briefly to let a yelping dog lunge at her. She always knew the exact limit of their leashes—and that she would never ever have to wear one. Then she flicked her tail and continued on.

Her name was Mau. She belonged to no one. No cats ever really do. They accept our offerings of food and devotion. They allow us to admire their beauty and copy their images for our amusement. We can only pretend to comprehend what goes on inside their minds. But we do know this. They are always thinking something intense and complex and extraordinary.

Mau moved purposefully, looking neither right nor left. She knew exactly where she was going. She didn't hurry; she had no need. Unlike the people and the cars rushing past her, she was supremely confident that the world would wait for her.

After crossing a narrow street and then a much busier and wider avenue, she stood on the sidewalk next to a dark gray stone wall. It was nearly ten times her height. She crouched down, twitched her tail several times, and then leapt to the top of the wall. She stood there for a moment. Was she admiring her own prowess? Or was she staring into what lay beyond?

And what was there? Trees, grass, playgrounds, baseball fields, hot dog vendors, benches, ponds, statues—in other words, all the ingredients of a park.

Central Park was beloved by New Yorkers for providing a respite of green from the dense concrete canyons. Much of the park had been sculpted to amuse the citizens. But there were still places that had not been touched. Tangled forests where wild animals lived. Murky ponds. And gigantic rocks that could have been the tops of mountains if they weren't buried in the ground.

Mau leapt off the wall and entered the dark, untamed heart of the city.

Was she hunting mice? Sparrows? Squirrels? Pigeons? She had feasted on them all. She preferred to find her own food, unless someone made an offering of a can of tuna. Putting the best parts of a great fish inside a small tin was mankind's greatest accomplishment. Or so it seemed to Mau.

She passed underneath several thickets of bushes and emerged in the shadow of great gray boulders flecked with shiny bits of quartz.

Two girls sprawled on top of the larger of the two rocks, surrounded by what was left of their lunches, their backpacks, and a bright yellow bag.

"Mau!" they cried.

Mau did them the honor of ignoring them. She sat at the base of the rock and licked her paw. When she first encountered the girls several years ago, she had avoided them completely. They didn't have any food she liked to eat. The things they called "goldfish" were actually small orange crackers. The other items were purposeless sweets; Mau didn't understand why humans enjoyed them so much.

"Hello, Mau. We hoped we'd see you." The girl called Val jumped down from the rock. She never sat still. She was always climbing or kicking a black-and-white ball that was too large to interest Mau.

But the other girl, the one called Lanora, was different. Mau spent a lot of time secretly observing her. Lanora wasn't a cat. She had no tail under her brightly colored skirt. And yet there was something about Lanora that Mau found to be familiar. Perhaps it was the intensity with which Lanora did absolutely nothing.

Mau walked through some bushes and reappeared on top of the rock, next to Lanora.

"Tomorrow is a very important day. There are very few times in our lives when we have the chance to begin again," Lanora said.

Val kicked the ball. It bounced off the base of the rock and returned so she could kick it again. "Whatever you wear will be fine."

"You don't have to think about it. You'll just wear a soccer shirt."

Mau sat on the rock about two feet from the edge of Lanora's skirt.

"And you are always comfortable in your own skin." Lanora smiled at Mau and held out her hand.

Mau sniffed the finger. She considered whether or not she wanted to be petted at that moment. She bowed her head and accepted a small scratch behind her ears. Then, because Lanora seemed agitated, Mau allowed her to slide her hand along Mau's sleek, black fur. Once, twice, three times—but no more. As it was, a great deal of bathing would be required to set things right.

"You fit your own skin, too," Val said.

Lanora shook her head. "I might be more like a snake. Or a hermit crab."

"Or a butterfly?" Val said.

Lanora opened the yellow bag. She held up a ring attached to a small, lilac-colored butterfly. Its antennae were threads. Its wings were plush fabric. Mau batted at it with her paw.

Val climbed up on the rock and took an orange butterfly out of the bag. She grabbed her backpack and examined the objects that dangled from a ring at its side. "We got puppies in third grade because we were sure we would get real ones that year."

"Instead my parents got divorced!" Lanora said with forced enthusiasm.

"Trolls in fourth grade," Val said.

"Because our teacher looked like one."

"Flashlights in fifth grade because we could finally walk all by ourselves to each other's apartment buildings."

"Except after dark."

"And butterflies this year because . . . how did you explain it?" Val said.

"It's time to stop crawling around on a leaf and fly."

Val clipped her orange butterfly to the ring with all the other dangles.

Lanora stared at hers as it lay limply on the palm of her hand. "Except these won't ever fly."

Val shook her backpack. The objects rattled but didn't fall. "Now I'm ready to start middle school."

Lanora said nothing.

Mau kept her eyes on Lanora's hand as she clenched the lilac butterfly in her fist.

Val picked up the trash from their lunch and stuffed everything in her backpack. "I'd better go home. Mom says if we want cookies, I have to help her. Don't worry, she won't let me mess them up too badly."

"I'm not worried," Lanora said.

"Are you coming, too?" Val said.

"I think I'll stay a little longer," Lanora said.

"Okay. See you tomorrow," Val said.

The two friends hugged. "'Bye, Mau." Val ran off through the park, kicking the ball as she went.

And so only Mau saw what Lanora did with the lilac butterfly.

New York City was on a grid. Lanora could remember the exact moment she figured this out. The boxes were rectangles instead of squares, but the numbered streets proceeded in order north and south. This was incredibly comforting, especially after her father moved out three years ago. She still knew where she was at all times. And even more importantly she knew where she was going.

After she left the park, she walked three blocks to what would be her new school. Middle School 10. The doors were locked. The brick walls refused to reveal secrets. That was okay. Lanora had already spent a lot of time studying a map of the new school. She wouldn't wander the halls with a lost look on her face. She would stride confidently from room to room, and sit in the seat she had chosen for herself—close to the windows in the third row. From there she could watch the other kids interact. There would be new kids, because M.S. 10 accepted students from several elementary schools. And so Lanora could pick totally new friends.

She continued on toward the apartment building where she lived with her mother. She didn't pass Val's building. If she wanted to walk to school with Val, Lanora would have to go four blocks out of her way. Val hadn't seemed to notice this important fact.

Lanora entered the lobby of her building. She took great care to step on the blue tiles of the floor and never the brown, even though she was a firm believer in making her own luck. There was an elevator, but it was so slow that Lanora always chose the stairs. As she climbed to the third floor, she considered her clothing options. Something fun and frivolous? Something dark and meaningful? Something eye-catching? Something aloof? Who did she want to be? She was troubled by her indecision.

In the past, she had always known what to wear. This was her particular kind of talent. She knew with the certainty of solving math problems what went with what. But she had never been in middle school before. The stakes were higher now.

"Lanora? Is that you?"

Her mother, Emma, was in the kitchen. Lanora came in and gave her a hug.

"Dinner is almost ready. I'm making fish. It's supposed to be brain food. Although why that would be, I have no idea."

"I like fish." Lanora smiled.

"I don't. It's so hard to get rid of the odor. For days after it's gone, you can still smell it."

The phone's sharp jangle pierced the room. Lanora let her mom answer.

"Hello? . . . Oh. It's you."

It was Lanora's father.

"Before you talk to her, I want to ask you. . . . I know you only have a few minutes, but this is important, too. . . . Then why don't you call when you do have time to talk? . . . I can't believe that you never have more than five minutes. . . . Yes, I have timed your conversations. . . . Because I wanted to be able to prove to you that you don't spend nearly enough time on your daughter . . ."

Lanora left the kitchen and went into her bedroom. She shut the door. She opened her window and swung her legs out over the sill so that her feet touched the metal slats of the fire escape. It was a law that each building in New York

City must provide an alternative exit, should disaster strike. There had never been a fire, thank goodness, and yet practically every day Lanora needed to escape.

The space between the apartment buildings was a deep pit. Lanora tried not to think about what was at its bottom. She wasn't afraid of heights; however, she was extremely afraid of falling. And so she clung to the metal bars even as she sat cross-legged on the platform and looked up toward the sky.

Two years ago, a thirty-story building had sprung up in the vacant lot behind them. It cast a permanent shadow across their apartment. Her mom had complained bitterly that the whole world was against her. But Lanora chose to imagine the future when she would be living in its penthouse. One night, while entertaining vivacious people, she would take one of the guests out to her balcony and point down down down.

"That's where I grew up," she would say.

"You sure have come a long way," the guest would say.

"Yes, I have."

But she wasn't there yet. A slight breeze reminded her that where she sat was more space than actual bars. She tightened her grip. Flecks of rust stuck to her sweaty hands. That wasn't reassuring. The air was eating away at the metal. Just like the doubts gnawing at Lanora's mind. She needed to decide what to wear.

Maybe she shouldn't have buried the butterfly dangle after Val left. What if that brought bad luck? But she couldn't just throw it away. And she certainly couldn't walk through the halls of her new middle school with a bunch of junk dangling from the bottom of her backpack. She couldn't even wear a backpack. She wanted to carry something sleek and black. Something that would command respect from everyone who saw it.

Lanora pulled herself up so that she stood on the platform. Her father was always telling her to make the hard choices. He said the difficult things were the only ones worth doing. She couldn't care less if some people didn't understand. She spoke out loud, so that the skyscraper could be her witness. "I have to do what I have to do."